MW00737477

A quality publisher of genre fiction.
Airdrie Alberta

Print ISBN 978-1-77299-128-4

2nd Edition
Copyright 2016 by Jude Pittman
Cover copyright 2016 by Michelle Lee

Dedication

Dedicated to my daughters
Judi-Ann Cartwright Smith (1965-2004)
Tami Cartwright
Billie Cartwright
Roxanne Pittman Nolan

Love Judy

Prologue

Kelly McWinter strode into the squad room of Fort Worth Special Ops. Except for the slight hitch in one of his long legs -- compliments of a gang banger who didn't appreciate having his meth lab shut down -- you'd never know the lanky Texan with the crooked smile and barely definable dimple in his chin, was a 13 year veteran of the Fort Worth PD.

"Hi Gil, Dan, everything ready?" Kelly nodded to his fellow officers.

"All set. Got the warrant right here," Dan Gallows patted his jacket pocket and picked up his automatic rifle.

"Command Central confirms there are four of them. Two in the front of the house and two back in the lab. They've only been cooking since noon, so they'll have to stay put the rest of the day.

"Okay." Kelly fastened his vest and buttoned up his jacket. We have two squad cars on standby they'll pick us up at the corner of Belknap and Knight and follow us to the clubhouse."

"We going in quiet?" Gil Martin asked as he stepped up beside his Chief.

"Dead silent. Remember, they'll be heavily armed and they aren't likely to go down easy."

* * *

Luckily the takedown went smooth as butter. They hit the clubhouse hard and fast, took all four by surprise, and never fired a shot. Gil and Dan crashed through the front door at the same instant that Kelly and Jeff Steuben from Patrol came through the back. The guards up front were having lunch and the two cooks in the back were sitting at a table playing cribbage. The Team had them down and cuffed before they could clear their heads enough to know they'd been breached.

* * *

Three weeks after the raid everything went to hell and Kelly's life exploded in a nightmare of flames and gut wrenching grief.

Someone leaked Kelly's home address to the bikers. They staked out his apartment and on a night when both Kelly and Lynda should have been attending a surprise party to celebrate Kelly's mentor, Jim Forbes' retirement from the force, they'd thrown a barrage of Molotov cocktails through the bedroom window. Kelly and Lynda had both planned to attend, but a couple hours before time to leave, Lynda got one of her migraines. Kelly had been torn between staying home with his sick wife and paying tribute to his mentor, but Lynda had insisted he attend the party. She'd already taken her pain medicine and by the time Kelly left she'd been sound asleep. He went alone.

Later, when he got the call to come home, the apartment building had burned to the ground. The fire chief told Kelly that the explosion had killed Lynda instantly. She'd never awoken and felt no pain. It was small consolation.

In the aftermath of the tragedy, Kelly resigned from the force, cut off all contact with his fellow officers and took a dead end job working security for a country flea market out in Indian Creek. He'd been there five years when murder brought him face to face with his past.

Chapter One

In the act of stepping through the front door at the Hideaway Bar and Barbecue, Kelly paused in mid-stride.

"You just try to throw me out of this cockroach-infested whorehouse." Anna Davis' shriek shattered the sound barrier.

Kelly had agreed to meet bar owner Cam Belcher for a couple of beers but if he'd known Anna was on one of her rampages, he'd have turned Cam's invitation down flat. He gritted his teeth, prepared to face the inevitable, and strolled across to the bar. A cloud of thick blue smoke cloaked the semi-dark room and Kelly aimed his eyes toward the sound of Anna's voice.

"Cam's got his hands full tonight." Darlene, Cam's barmaid, stopped beside Kelly and pointed across the room to where a scrawny little woman in an old black poncho had Cam backed as far up against the pool table as he could get without settling his backside onto the felt.

"Sure looks that way," Kelly agreed. "Bring me a cool one, will you? I've got a feeling I'm going to need a couple of them."

Turning back to watch the show, Kelly was just in time to catch Cam's eye. "Help!" the desperate barman mouthed a plea. With a resigned shrug, Kelly swung his leg off the barstool and headed across the room.

"What's wrong with my best gal?" Kelly moved in front of Anna and blocked her view of Cam.

"Stupid jackass says I can't hold my whiskey." Anna lifted her head and wobbled unsteadily.

"Whoa. Steady now." Kelly reached out to catch her shoulders just as she lurched and landed flat against his chest. Giggling, she tilted her head and gave him a drunken smile.

Kelly sighed and tightened his arm around her shoulders. He liked Anna a lot, even if she was a drunk. "Easy now."

He took her arm and steered her toward a table where Bubba Tate and Leroy Elliott were set up with one of those giant bottles of whiskey the locals referred to as Texas Mickies.

"How's it going, boys?" Kelly nodded to Bubba and Leroy.

"Hey, Kelly!" Bubba grinned at Kelly and reached over to pull out a chair. "How ya doin'?"

"Not bad." Kelly helped Anna into the chair and rested his arm along the backrest.

Bubba, a bowlegged, potbellied shorty with the face of a mischievous boy, pushed his cowboy hat back on his forehead and pointed at the bottle. "Care for a shot?"

"Thanks, I'll pass but Anna could probably do with one," Kelly picked up a glass and handed it across the table. "I'm going over to have a chat with Cam, so how about you boys keep her company for a spell?"

"You bet!" Bubba grabbed the bottle. "She was sitting here with me'n Leroy before her and Cam got mixing it up." Bubba poured a healthy shot into Anna's glass.

"Good!" Kelly patted Anna's arm and turned away.

At the bar, Cam had his head bent over a sink full of soapsuds. "Time for a break," Kelly shouted over the clamor of voices.

Cam grabbed the towel from around his neck and wiped his hands. "You bet, this place has been nuts all night. Guess you noticed, Anna's on one of her benders."

Kelly grinned. "Yep, got that okay. Why not let Darlene take over for a while and we'll go out on the patio." Kelly nodded his head toward the back of the room.

"Sure thing." Cam waved a hand to get Darlene's attention. "I'm going to step outside with Kelly for a spell."

"Gotcha, boss."

Cam grabbed a couple of longnecks out of the cooler and followed Kelly outside. The patio—added after his folks retired—was Cam's pride and joy. The fancy barbecue pit, charcoal smoker and raised platform stage had been an instant hit and the row of outdoor booths flanking the stage allowed non-smokers like Kelly an opportunity to join the fun while still preserving their lungs.

"So, what's going on with you and Anna?" Kelly folded his legs into one of the booths and accepted a beer.

"Not me. She's been like this ever since she came in from the flea market."

Kelly frowned. "What did she mean by that crack about you throwing her out?"

Cam flushed. "I was just tryin' some damage control. You know how she gets when she starts on the whiskey. She started raisin' hell with Bubba and I knew it was only a matter of time before she exploded and there'd be furniture flyin'."

"Hopefully, Bubba and Leroy will keep her occupied for a while. In any event, the way she's pouring it back, she won't last long."

Cam brushed his hair back off his forehead and sighed. "She's hard to take when she gets on the hard stuff. I'll give her another hour or two, then get Darlene to walk her home. She handles Anna better than I do."

"There was a young gal at the flea market earlier today who got into some kind of ruckus with Anna. Maybe that had something to do with the mood she's in?"

"What happened?"

"I'm not sure. It seems the girl knocked Anna out of her chair. I wouldn't have known anything about it if the girl hadn't caught my eye when she first came into the flea market."

"A looker?"

"As a matter of fact, she was. But what got my attention was the way she edged into the flea market. Almost like she was hiding from someone."

"A street kid?"

"Not at all. She looked like she belonged over at Lake Country estates—classy dresser."

"Wonder what she wanted with Anna?"

"That's what I've been trying to figure out. She stuck out like a sore thumb the way she kept darting looks over her shoulder. Of course that made me curious enough to start following her, but she spotted me quick enough."

"Getting careless in your old age?"

Kelly laughed. "You know what it's like on Saturday afternoons with the kids running up and down the aisles and mom and pop keeping one eye on them and the other peeled for bargains. I tried not to be obvious but I had to get close just to keep her in sight and that's what spooked her. As soon as she realized I was following her, she ducked into the refreshment stand."

"Maybe she thought you were stalking her."

"Nope. She came in the door watching her back. Anyway, I ducked behind Luis' patio and watched her after she went inside the refreshment stand. She darted into that little kitchen where Luis steams his tamales, then ducked out again. I had a good view from where I stood, so I stayed put and kept my eye on her. She watched the crowd for a while, looking for me probably, then she started edging up toward Anna's stall."

"Was anybody in the stall besides Anna?"

"Not at first but Bubba came along while the girl was watching. It was right after he showed up she went into her act."

"It sounds more like you and Bubba set her off than Anna. Hell, she might've been an out-of-town collector going to Anna's stall on business. You gotta look at it from her point of view. First she spots this long, tall country dude with a knowing look in his eye following her down the aisle and she no sooner ditches him than she runs smack into a sawed-off shrimp with exactly the same kinda knowing look in his eye."

Kelly chuckled. "Frankly, I'd be inclined to chalk it up to a bad case of the jitters if it wasn't for the way Anna acted after the whole thing was over."

"How's that?"

"Like I said, I wasn't sure about her intentions so when she started edging toward Anna's stall, I moved in a little closer. I'd just about reached the entrance when the girl lit into a run, made a flying leap across the aisle and straight into the stall. I hopped on it then and made it to the door just in time to see Anna's rocker tipping ass over tea kettle. Dumped the girl face down on the floor and spilled Anna on top of her."

"I bet Anna was chewing nails."

"That's the funny part. The woman was out cold but Anna was okay. When I picked Anna up and dusted her off, I expected she'd cuss that gal up one side and down the other but she never said a thing. Not one single word. She just sat back down in that rocker, turned her eyes onto the girl and kept them there. I swear to God, Cam, she acted like she'd seen a ghost."

"You figure Anna knew the girl?"

"Either that or there was something going on between them that I didn't pick up on. The girl came around while I was watching Anna. Before I knew it, she'd taken off out the door and disappeared into the crowd."

"Strange," Cam shook his head.

"Yeah, it's got my curiosity piqued. I'm going to wait until Bubba sobers up and see if he knows anything about her."

"Good plan." Cam nodded agreement. "By the way, where'd Jake get to?"

"Oh, he was off somewhere when I left— probably chasing squirrels again—so I came without him."

Jake was Kelly's dog, or as Kelly liked to put it, Jake was a dog and the question of who was master hadn't been decided. The black-and-tan German shepherd with one ragged ear and enough scars to show he'd been around was all the family Kelly had left now that Lynda and his mom were both dead.

Jake must have had his ESP turned on because Cam had no sooner asked about him than he came bounding through the gate and up the steps of the patio.

"About time you put in an appearance." Kelly reached out to stroke the dog's head.

Jake slapped his tail against Kelly's leg and walked over to shove his nose into Cam's outstretched hand.

"He's probably been out ridding the woods of dangerous squirrels," Cam said, running an affectionate hand along Jake's ribs.

"I guess at least one of us needs to get some exercise." Kelly unwound his six-foot frame from the booth and stretched to loosen a few muscles.

"Well, I guess it's time to get back to work," Cam said, standing up beside Kelly. "Wish me luck with Anna."

"It'd be nice if I could say things will probably settle down around here." Kelly stepped over to the railing and tilted his head to look up at the sky. "But it's a full moon out there and I'm afraid it's going to be one of those nights."

The two of them peered up through the pecan trees to where the moon—plump and rich in its fullness—bathed the branches in gleaming silver.

"What's that old superstition about pale riders and moonlit nights?" Kelly grinned and closed his eye in a teasing wink.

"Don't even joke about stuff like that." Cam shuddered and shook himself as if to ward off an evil eye.

Chapter Two

Back at the cabin Kelly stretched out in his recliner and dozed. At one-thirty, when the alarm buzzed for his two o'clock rounds at the flea market, he woke to find a storm had rolled in while he slept.

Kelly swiped the steaming window and squinted at the steady stream of rain that poured off the eaves. "Looks like a real gully washer, Jake."

Jake hated storms. He paced anxiously back and forth from the front door to the kitchen.

"You might as well settle down. We aren't going out in that stuff. Kelly picked up the coffee pot and flicked the switch for brew. He pulled a chair up to the kitchen table. When the coffee finished, he poured a cup and watched as a faint glimmer of light broke through the clouds. Giant maples thick with darkening leaves leaned across the path to the flea market. By two o'clock the winds had receded. "Looks like it's about blown itself out, Jake." Kelly pulled on his boots and grabbed a slicker out of the closet.

Jake raced across the room and stood expectantly in front of the door.

"Okay, I get it," Kelly chuckled. "Let's get on down there and get it over with."

Inside the barn housing the flea market, the beam from Kelly's flashlight danced over sheet-covered tables. These tables were for short-term vendors who rented from Friday to Sunday and covered their goods with sheets when they left for the night.

Permanent dealers had their own shops, enclosed three-sided cubicles with curtained entrances where they sold everything from old standbys like hats, boots, jeans and t-shirts to gaudy jewelry and swirling salsa dresses. Then there were the new and used shops, like Anna's, where treasure hunters could browse through boxes of ornamental plates, old glasses and beer steins and baskets overflowing with everything from spoon collections to buttons and badges dating back to the Civil War.

Kelly and Jake walked along the aisles. Gusts of wind whipped across the shrouded tables and buffeted the sheets into dancing ghosts. The barn steamed with moisture left by the storm and Kelly itched to complete his rounds. He had an edgy feeling that made him anxious to get out of the barn. Jake seemed to feel it too. He paced the concrete, ears perked and alert, as if listening for something half expected.

When they finally turned into the last aisle, Kelly breathed a sigh of relief and quickened his pace. The refreshment stand, dimly lit by a Budweiser neon guitar cut in the shape of the state of Texas, loomed ahead in the shadows.

Jake had trotted ahead. He stopped and lifted his nose, then pulled back his lips and let out a menacing growl. Kelly clicked the flashlight on high and trained it into the refreshment stand. Inside, an old refrigerator leaned against the wall and a silver coffee urn glinted on the counter.

Kelly moved the light across the stand and on the ground in front of the door. The light picked out a dark bundle that looked like rags. Kelly focused the light and started forward, moving fast. When he reached a spot where the light sharpened the shadows into images, the bundle became a body and a sharp odor—the kind you never forgot—stung his nostrils.

"My God!" He sprinted the distance to the booth, Jake hard on his heels.

Kelly recognized the old, black poncho. Instinct told him what to expect. He dropped to his knees, reached out and pulled back the poncho. Jake stiffened and growled.

Anna Davis' pupils were rolled back under swollen lids. Her blood-gorged tongue filled her mouth. Kelly fought waves of nausea and gulped air. His hands clenched into fists. It only took a couple of minutes for him to pull himself together and get to his feet.

"Let's go, boy." He cleared his throat with a strangled cough. "We've got some calls to make."

Jake fell into step and they crossed to the box in front of the refreshment stand. Kelly flipped the master switch. Bright light flooded the barn and spilled across Anna. Jake growled and Kelly stroked his head. "Easy now." He settled his hand on Jake's back. "I need to call the county." Kelly pulled the phone out of his pocket and dialed the Tarrant County Sheriff's Department.

Seconds later, a crisp efficient voice said hello.

"This is Kelly McWinter. Security guard at the Indian Creek Flea Market. And I've got a dead body inside I just found on my two o'clock walk-through."

"Routing a patrol car now, sir. Please wait for them.

"My cabin's up at the entrance. I'll open the gates and wait out front for it to get here." Kelly pocketed his phone and turned to Jake. "Come on boy, let's get up the hill."

At thirty-eight Kelly still had the smooth, well-paced gait of an athlete and only a practiced eye would notice the stiffness in his left leg—a souvenir from a stray bullet.

All clouds had been swirled away by the storm's wind and now moonlight bathed the cabin in an eerie gray and orange glow, fitting for this night. Kelly opened the main gates and headed for the cabin. He settled into an old rocker on the porch to wait. Jake flopped at his feet. Silence covered the flea market like a blanket. Even the crickets were still. Mechanically, Kelly set the chair to rocking. Pictures of Anna flashed through his mind, a kaleidoscope of memories tracing the years he'd spent at Indian Creek.

Time passed and in the distance a siren sounded. Kelly squinted northward and spotted flashes of red and blue lights. Minutes later, a patrol car turned into the yard and pulled up to the cabin.

A young deputy, just a kid with short blonde hair trimmed close to his ears, jumped from the car and strode to the porch. His brown and tan uniform was immaculate.

"Are you Kelly McWinter? I'm Deputy Johnson." He didn't wait for an answer. "I understand you've got a body here."

"That's right." Kelly rose and crossed the porch to meet the officer. "She's down by the refreshment stand. I checked to make sure she was dead."

Johnson narrowed his eyes. His right hand, resting on the butt of his holstered gun, stiffened.

"Nobody ever tell you not to touch a corpse?"

Kelly smiled. He remembered the first time he'd been called out on a homicide.

"Hey, it's all right." He kept his voice low and friendly. "I used to be on the force myself. I know the drill."

Johnson relaxed a bit but kept his hand on the holster. "Okay, just so's you didn't contaminate anything."

The county ambulance pulled up with squealing tires. Two men in white overalls jumped out. A veteran with stooped shoulders and a mop of thick gray hair climbed into the back of the van and handed a large black case to a well-muscled, young Mexican.

Johnson walked over to the van, said a few words, and signaled Kelly to lead the way down the hill.

Kelly took them in through the double doors and approached the refreshment stand.

"Over there." He pointed.

The younger medic stepped into the circle of light that beamed from the ceiling, set his case beside Anna's feet and started unpacking.

"Watch what the hell you're doing?" The harsh voice boomed through the silent barn. The young medic startled and tumbled into Anna's cash box. It skidded across the cement.

A stocky cop with short legs and long arms stomped onto the scene. "Can't you see this is a friggin' crime scene?" The cop's thick, bulbous nose quivered and his cheeks puffed out. The red-faced medic bent to retrieve his case and the cop turned to Kelly.

"I'm Sergeant Adams," he said. "You the guy that reported this?"

"That's right. I'm the security guard here. I found her when I made my two o'clock rounds."

"Okay, I'll get to you in a minute."

Adams was a hard ass but Kelly sympathized. If there was any chance Anna was still alive, the medics would have priority at the scene. But there wasn't any chance and plenty of vital evidence could be destroyed in the first few minutes of an investigation. An over-anxious medic was the defense attorney's best friend. They'd been known to smear fingerprints, brush off hair and fibers and wipe away any sign of bodily fluids. Kelly'd seen it all, including an over-anxious medic starting CPR on a cold corpse.

Adams and Johnson stood over the body, talking in low voices. Kelly watched as Adams bent down, lifted the poncho then dropped it back in place.

"Only an idiot would think there was any life left in that," he snapped and turned back to Johnson. "Go call the CID, then wait out front to show the lab boys where to bring their stuff."

He turned to the medics. "You might as well get your shit out of here," he growled. "You can stick around out front until the coroner arrives, then shove off."

The senior medic, an old-timer who looked like he'd been through this before, shrugged and motioned to his partner to step away from the body. Johnson pulled his cell out of his pocket and pressed a button to call the criminal investigations division, a team of forensic experts and the county coroner.

Kelly walked over to Adams stood, frowning at Anna's body.

"Tell me what you know about this. Let's sit down over there." Adams turned and marched over to one of the picnic tables. Kelly rolled his eyes and followed him. Adams slid onto one of the benches and Kelly eased his long frame onto the other one.

Adams took out a notebook.

Kelly propped his arm on the table and turned his mind back to the start of his rounds. Jake, who'd stood back from the group of strangers, padded over, sank down and rested his nose on Kelly's boot.

"I was doing last rounds," Kelly said. "That'd make it about two o'clock when Jake here raised his hackles and started growling."

Jake heard his name and lifted his eyes to the sergeant.

"You don't know Jake." Kelly reached down and stroked the dog's head. "He doesn't make a fuss without a reason, so I was edgy. There's not much goes on around here after the barn's closed up but sometimes we get kids messing around. This wasn't like that though. Jake knows the difference between kids and trouble and something was damn sure setting him off."

"Whereabouts were you when this happened?"

"About half way down that aisle." Kelly pointed toward the last row of tables. "At first I couldn't see anything but when I trained my flashlight on the refreshment stand, I spotted what looked like a bundle of rags dropped in the aisle. I clicked the beam on high and that's when I recognized Anna's poncho."

"Did you hear anything?"

24

"Nope, not a sound, except Jake here. He was riled something fierce."

"Okay, then what?"

"Well, like I said, I recognized that old, black poncho of Anna's. She wore it all the time. So I took off down the aisle like a bat out of hell. The poncho was wrapped around her face and I pulled it off. That was tough." Kelly squeezed his eyes shut for a moment. Then he continued. "There was a red scarf sunk so deep in her neck, I thought she'd been slashed."

"Did you touch the scarf?"

"Just the edge. I pulled her skin back a bit, to make sure but there wasn't a chance. Then I headed for the phone, got the county dispatcher and gave her the details, and Jake and I went to the cabin to wait for your deputy."

"You got any ideas who did this?"

Kelly shook his head. "Just the obvious one that comes to mind from seeing her cash box broken open and coins scattered around the ground." Kelly leaned across the table and fixed his eyes on Adams' face. "It don't make a lot of sense, y'know? If all he wanted was money, why kill her? For that matter, what was she doing prowling around down here at that time of night?"

"He?" Adams questioned.

"He...her...whatever. I guess strangling's kind of fixed in my mind as something a man would do."

"Do you know of anybody who might've had it in for Ms. Davis?"

"Hell, no. Anna was kind of an eccentric. She drank like a fish, ate like a bird and God only knows how old she was. I liked her a lot but she was a bit of a tartar, especially when she'd been hitting the bottle. Still, I can't see any of the Indian Creek folks having it in for her. They pretty much took Anna in their stride."

"We'll be wanting a list of her friends and associates from you. Deputy Johnson will attend to that. In the meantime, it'd help if you could think of someone who might know about anything out of the ordinary happening around here."

"Well, these folks are pretty closed-mouthed with strangers but you might talk to Frank Perkins. You'll find him either up at the Hideaway or down at the bait house. If anybody farts on the creek, Frank knows all the details."

Adams looked up from his notebook and nodded. "We'll talk to him. What about strangers? Was there anybody who paid particular attention to Anna or asked a lot of questions about her?"

"Anna had a bit of a ruckus with one of the shoppers over at her stall this afternoon."

Adams lifted his head and fixed his eyes on Kelly. "Tell me about it."

"There was a young woman showed up here about four o'clock. A real looker. For some reason, this woman rushed into Anna's shop and flung herself right on top of Anna's chair. I don't know whether it was deliberate or not. All I know is when I got there, both Anna and the woman were tangled up on the floor and the woman was out cold."

"Did you recognize her?"

"Nope. She wasn't from around here, not the flea market type. I figured she might've been an antique collector. Anna had a lot of collectibles in her stall."

"Description?"

"She was around twenty-five, about five-six, around a hundred and ten pounds, plenty of curves in all the right places. Her hair was long and silky and so blonde it was almost white. She wore it straight down her back, held in place with one of those silk scarves."

Adams scribbled in his book. Finished, he looked up and nodded. "Go ahead."

"I spotted her soon after she came through the front entrance. She was a knockout. That's what drew my eye. But then I noticed the way she acted. It was kind of funny."

"What do you mean by funny? You mean drunk?"

"No, nothing like that. More like she was trying to hide from somebody. She kept looking back over her shoulder and when she realized I had my eye on her, she scooted into the crowd like a flushed quail. Her whole manner was suspicious. That's why I followed her down to Anna's."

"Did you happen to notice if anybody was paying any special attention to this woman? Is it possible she was being followed?"

"Nope. Nobody paid her any more attention than what she'd normally get, given her looks and figure."

Adams jotted a few more lines in the book then twirled his pen again.

"The woman?" Adams nudged.

"I kept my eye on her but didn't make it obvious. When she got next to the refreshment stand, she stopped for a bit and stood there looking kind of nervous. She'd pulled the scarf out of her hair and was kneading it with her fingers."

"What color was that scarf?"

Kelly nodded. "I know where you're going with that," he said. "It was red and yes, it could've been the one that's wrapped around Anna's neck. I'd have a hard time swearing to it though. I didn't give it more than a casual glance at the time."

Kelly paused and Adams tapped his pen on the table. "What happened next?"

"Not much. I got there right after she and Anna went down. The fall knocked her out and after I got Anna back in her chair, I turned to talk to the young woman. She'd gotten to her feet by then."

"Did you get her name?"

Kelly shook his head. "She took off before I had a chance."

"You let her go without asking any questions?"

"I wasn't thinking about questions at that point. I needed to check Anna out and make sure she was okay. Besides, she hadn't done anything except fall into a chair."

"What did Anna have to say?"

"Not a damn thing. I picked her up, brushed off her dress and asked her what happened. She wouldn't say a word, just looked up at me with those big brown eyes of hers, set her teeth on her lip and tuned me out."

"Did you get the impression Ms. Davis knew the young woman?"

"I don't know. There was something going on between them but as to whether it was recognition or just plain shock, I couldn't say." Kelly stood up and shook down his pant legs. "That's all I can tell you. I'd never seen the woman before and I don't expect you'll find anybody around here who had. Now, if you're through with me I'd like to get back to my cabin. I need to call the owner and let him know what's been going on."

Adams closed his notebook. "Okay, go ahead but keep yourself available."

Kelly nodded, signaled Jake and they headed up the hill.

Kelly's first priority was a pot of coffee. That done, he picked up the phone and dialed Shorty.

"I've got one hell of a mess out here," he said when Shorty's voice came on the line.

"Wad'ya mean, mess?"

"Someone's murdered Anna."

"Murdered. What're you talking about? I thought you were supposed to be down at the barn making rounds?"

"Where the hell do you think I've been? I found Anna's body in there about two hours ago. Some son of a bitch had taken a scarf and damn near squeezed her head off."

Kelly's hands tightened on the phone. The events of the night had taken their toll. He moved the receiver away from his mouth took a deep breath, flexed his shoulders then put the phone back to his ear. "Sorry, Shorty. I guess I'm stretched too tight."

The anger in Shorty's voice had been replaced with concern. "Not a problem, Kelly. Sounds like you've had one hell of a night. Do you want me to come over and give you a hand?"

"No. There's nothing you can do now. The place is crawling with cops. I've already told them everything I know. I'll just grab some coffee and wait until they've finished up down below."

"You'll make sure they lock up once they get done in there?"

"Don't worry about that. They'll seal the place up tight. I'll make sure though."

Hanging up the phone, Kelly eased out of his chair and stretched. His hands grazed the ceiling and he flexed his fingers against the tile.

"It doesn't look like we'll get much sleep tonight," he muttered to Jake. "Guess we might as well make ourselves comfortable while those boys take care of business."

Coffee mug in hand, Kelly pulled out one of the kitchen chairs and parked himself at the scarred, old oak table he kept in front of the window. Several cars had arrived while he was on the phone. He leaned against the window and watched an old geezer unload a stretcher out of the back of the coroner's wagon.

Jake curled up at Kelly's feet. He rested his snout between his paws but he kept a close eye on the front door and his ears perked, on full alert.

Time dragged. Kelly moved across to the black leather couch and stretched out to wait for Adams to let him know when to lock up again. Kelly drifted into a restless sleep. Jake's bark startled him awake several hours later.

"What's up?" His feet hit the floor and he was off the couch in one smooth motion.

Knuckles rapped against the door and Jake started to growl.

"Easy, boy," Kelly soothed the dog as he strode across the room and opened the door.

"Well, I'll be a son of a bitch," a loud gravelly voice greeted Kelly's stunned face. "I called Adams a damn liar when he told me who'd called this one in."

Kelly stood and gaped at the large black man filling his doorway. "Gus!" Finding his tongue, Kelly reached out and threw his arms around the solid, burly form of his old friend and former partner.

Augustus Graham—known to only a few very good friends as Gus—returned the hug. "I knew you'd moved out of the city but we hadn't heard from you in so long, I'd given you up for lost," he said.

Kelly nodded toward the table. "Have a seat. I'll grab you a coffee."

Gus moved across the room and took a chair, while Kelly stepped into the kitchen.

"Coffee's been on for a while, so it ought to be just right for you." Kelly set a large mug on the table and pulled out the other chair. "Damn, it's good to see you."

Gus took a swig and propped his elbows on the table. "Some of the guys were hurt when you dropped out of sight the way you did, but I understood. Like as not I've have done the same if it had been Betty instead of Lynda."

Kelly flinched at Lynda's name but Gus kept talking. "I always figured you for a city boy, never expected to find you down here with the Creek rats. What's it been? Four or five years?"

"Five. Sometimes I can't believe it myself. I guess I needed to get clean away from everything once the trial was over."

"That was rough."

"It's not that I was trying to duck you guys. I just couldn't help it. Every time I saw one of you guys with your wives, I went nuts. There were just too many memories. I had to buy myself some time to deal with them."

"I know." Gus' voice caught and he coughed, loudly clearing his throat. "I've missed you," he said, fingers drumming the table.

"Thanks, Gus. I'm dealing with the past a little easier now but it's still raw. Maybe one of these days we can take on a couple of platters of ribs over at Angeles and sort of catch up on things."

"Sounds good." Gus smacked his lips. "I haven't had a plate of those ribs since I left the city. My mouth is watering just thinking about them."

Gus shifted back in his chair and the atmosphere changed. It was time to get down to business. "So, what can you tell me about that woman down there?" he asked and jerked his head toward the window.

"I can't tell you a hell of a lot more than what I've already told your associates." Kelly shook his head. "Have you been briefed?"

Gus nodded.

"Then you've already got everything I know. Once the Hideaway opens, there'll be a bunch of the flea market crowd in for morning coffee. I'll wander over and see if anybody knows anything."

Gus lifted an eyebrow. "Don't go forgetting you're a civilian."

Kelly grinned. "I won't."

"Okay." Gus rose from the chair. "I'll probably want to talk to you later but you might as well get some shuteye while we're finishing up. I'll have someone give you a holler when they get done down there."

"Thanks, Gus. I'll catch a few winks while I wait for the Hideaway to open. Nice seeing you again."

"Yeah." Gus headed for the door. "Been too damn long."

Kelly went back to the couch. Hours later, a hard knock brought him to his feet. He glanced at the clock. Its hands sat on eight-thirty. He pulled open the door. Deputy Johnson stood on the porch.

"We're about wrapped up," Johnson said, his voice heavy with fatigue. "We've taped it off, so be sure you keep everyone away until we see if there's anything more to be done down there."

Kelly nodded. "I'll post a notice and lock up the gates. Sunday's a big day at the flea market but I reckon that's Shorty's problem. Thanks for letting me know."

After the last patrol car pulled out of the lot, Kelly hiked down the hill, ducked under the police tape, checked the padlock and flipped the switch to kill the lights.

"Let's go see what's going on at the Hideaway," he said. He signaled Jake and the two of them started up the hill.

On the bridge, Kelly stopped. Up the hill, the Hideaway's parking lot was full. The Indian Creek grapevine worked fast and there'd be a barrage of questions when Kelly walked in the door. Leaning over the rail, he took a couple of deep breaths to let the tension seep out of his muscles.

The storm had settled the dust and plumped the air with a spicy tang. Kelly breathed deeply and exhaled slowly. Gus had been right. He was a city boy but the past five years had sucked the caffeine and adrenaline out of his bones. The burning anger left in the aftermath of Lynda's death had dulled somewhat. It never went away—probably never would—but at least he'd learned to live with it.

But in the wake of last night's tragedy, Kelly could feel the old impulses resurfacing. The knot was back in his gut and he wasn't sure whether that was a bad thing or not.

Chapter Three

It was Sunday morning and Tarrant County had a law against serving liquor before noon, so the crowd in the Hideaway was strictly coffee and gossip.

On the front porch, Kelly took a deep breath and prepared for the onslaught. The thirst for blood and gore he found in ordinary people turned his stomach a bit. As a cop he'd gotten used to it but he'd been away from all that for a while. He'd have to reorient himself because there was nothing like feeding those appetites to get the tongues wagging.

Kelly gave the door a shove and the high, quavering voice of Doug Phillips caught him mid-stride.

"I heard it was Anna that got it down there. Is that who it was?"

Kelly cringed. He wasn't about to let Phillips latch onto him. The cantankerous old bugger's breath stank like a silo.

"Yeah, it was Anna," Kelly growled.

Phillips grinned, showing a mouthful of rotten teeth. "See, I told y'all it was Anna," he gloated to the old farts at his table. "Got herself strangled is what I heard. Ain't that right, Kelly?"

Making no attempt to hide his distaste, Kelly snapped back. "I said it was Anna. Now I came in here for a cup of coffee, so let me get settled."

Jake didn't like Phillips. He'd hung back while the old man asked his questions. Now he edged around Kelly and padded over to the potbellied heater in the center of the room. He sank down on the metal pad that protected the wood floor from errant sparks and settled in for a well-deserved nap.

Kelly grabbed a mug from the shelf, helped himself to the coffee pot and settled into a booth. Cam came out of the kitchen with a load of mugs and waved a hand. Kelly nodded back.

Conversation hummed at the round table. Kelly leaned back and let it buzz over his head. His cop's ear would pick up anything relevant. The rest was just noise.

Cam set to work polishing the counter tops and Kelly watched the barman. A husky, six-footer with broad shoulders and the beginning of a paunch, Cam could usually be counted on for a cheerful "howdy" and a welcoming smile. Not today. Tension showed in the rigid set of his jaw and the quick snap of towel against vinyl.

Anna'd died at the flea market but she'd spent most of the night at the Hideaway. Cops weren't good for the bar business and Cam would be worried about the backlash.

Kelly understood Cam's feelings. The Hideaway was the barman's pride and joy. Stepping inside was like taking a trip down memory lane. The décor—a tribute to the owner's passion for country music and country living—was a potpourri of tools and implements from the turn of the century. Cam proudly displayed his collection of antique beer wagons in a glass case behind the bar. His piece-de-resistance was the cherished replica of the Budweiser Clydesdales rigged out in full harness.

Even the ceiling bore witness to Cam's passion. Glossy black and white photos of Hank Williams, Patsy Cline, Faron Young and a whole slew of long-dead country favorites smiled down on the patrons.

An argument broke out at the round table and Phil Morley's high soprano caught Kelly's ear.

"I bet you they was after her money," Phil squeaked. "I remember Frank saying she had half a million bucks stashed out here somewhere."

"Aw, Frank's full of shit," Doug Phillips scoffed. "I heard that crap too but I figured it for another one of his fish tales."

"I don't know," Jim Spencer broke in. "I heard the same story and it didn't come from Frank either. Rumor has it she loaned Cam a pile of dough to keep this place going. There probably isn't nothin' like half a million but I bet there's a good-sized stash."

Doug twirled his hand at Cam for another round for the table. "Maybe so," he turned back to the group, "but I'd have to see it to believe it. Anyway, even if Anna did have that kind of money, she sure as hell didn't bury it in the ground. She may have been a drunk but she wasn't stupid."

Cam leaned over the table and set down a tray loaded with steaming mugs and Doug grabbed one. "I wonder where the hell she came from." He shook his head when nobody spoke up. "I don't think even Bubba knows anything about her past."

"It's like I always said..." Jim paused with a mug held midair, "she was married to some rich dude and when she started hitting the bottle, he kicked her ass out."

"Maybe we ought to go down to her cabin and take a look around," Phil said.

"You got to be off your rocker!" Doug choked and spurted coffee across the table. "There'll be cops all over that place. You stick one foot inside her cabin and they'll haul your ass off to jail and hang a murder rap on you. Them cops don't give a shit who killed the old hag. They just want to get her off their books so they can go back to writing tickets."

"Doug's right." Jim nodded. "We'd all better stay the hell away from Anna's cabin. When the cops start askin' questions, we don't know nothin'. Cops got a nose for money and if they once get the idea Anna had something buried out here, we'll never get 'em off our ass."

A sharp cough brought Kelly's head around. Cam stood beside the booth clutching a bar towel.

"Sorry, Cam, I didn't notice you there." Kelly pulled in his legs. "I guess the lack of sleep's catching up with me."

"No problem." Cam smiled and swiped his towel across the table. "I was wondering if you could spare an hour or so. I've got some stuff I need to get off my chest."

"Sure. I've got plenty of time on my hands now the cops have locked up the flea market."

"Thanks." Cam gave the table a last flick of the towel. "We'll go to my place as soon as Darlene shows up. I don't want that bunch listening in." He waved his arm toward the group at the round table.

Kelly nodded. "Gimme a yell when you're ready. Meantime, I'll grab another coffee."

Jake, who'd apparently had enough of the stove, edged past Kelly when he got up to refill his cup and trotted down the wooden steps to the back lot. Kelly grinned. The lot was heaven for a dog. Mice, rabbits, squirrels and cats chased each other through the tangled roots and branches of honeysuckles and lilacs.

The outside door swung open and Bubba Tate stepped into the room.

"You okay?" Kelly crossed the floor and met him halfway.

"I can't take it in, Kelly," Bubba said. "Anna was with me 'n Leroy 'til somewhere around midnight and now she's dead."

"I know, Bubba." Kelly put his arm around the little guy's shoulders and led him over to the booth.

"You know we had a spat last night?" Bubba kept talking, his mind too overwhelmed to think of anything but Anna. "She stomped outta here mad as the devil but you know Anna. She'd done that lots of times. I just figured she'd gone to the house. Then this morning, they woke me up and told me somebody killed her. I shoulda been with her, Kelly. She'd still be alive if I hadn't been such an asshole."

"Hey!" Kelly squeezed Bubba's shoulder. "There's no point blaming yourself. Come on, let's go sit down and talk a spell."

Bubba slid into the booth. "You know what it was like before you left. We were sharing that Texas mickey of Jack Daniels Shorty'd given to Leroy and weren't none of us feeling any pain."

"That much I noticed."

Bubba shook his head and looked sheepish. "Leroy and I'd both noticed how het up Anna was," he said, "but we figured the whiskey'd tame her down. It didn't seem to be working though. The more she drank, the meaner she got. When Cam told her to get her ass on home, she went nuts."

Kelly frowned. "I thought that had all been settled before I left. They didn't start in again, did they?"

"It was Leroy got it started. He was pretty tanked up and Anna musta said somethin' to set him off. I was talkin' to Doug Phillips at the time, so I didn't hear what he said. But whatever it was, it started Anna right back in on Cam again."

Kelly gave a disgusted shake of his head. "Trust Leroy to start his mouth going without stoppin' to put his brain in gear."

"Yep, that's the home boy all right." Bubba laughed and tugged at his cowboy hat. "You shoulda seen the look on Anna's face. She yelled out somethin' about screwin' Cam and the horse he rode in on and that pulled my attention away from Doug in a hurry. I took one look and figured sure as hell she was gonna let loose again. That's when I came back to the table and I guess I made kind of an ass of myself."

Kelly raised his eyebrow and Bubba's face flushed then he pulled the brim of his cowboy hat down and coughed a couple of times. "I could usually kid Anna out of one of her moods but not last night. I don't know what was biting her but she sure wasn't acting like herself. Even Leroy noticed it. She had something stuck in her craw and I don't think it had a damn thing to do with Cam telling her to git on home."

"She didn't mention anything about that gal in the flea market, did she?"

Bubba shook his head. "Nope, not a word. You think there was something funny about that?"

"Not necessarily. I just thought it was odd the way Anna handled the whole thing."

"Well, she didn't say anything to me. Matter of fact, she didn't talk much at all, except to cuss Cam up one side and down the other."

"So you figure it was about midnight when Anna left the bar?"

"Near as I can recollect it was. We'd put a pretty good dent in the bottle and everything was friendly enough but then like I said, I moved over and was talkin' to Doug and the boys. That's when Leroy got Anna riled up again."

Kelly frowned. "So neither you nor Leroy offered to go with her when she was ready to leave."

"She'd have decked me if I'd tried to go home with her," Bubba muttered.

"I thought her beef was with Cam."

Bubba blushed. "I told you I acted like a jerk."

Kelly scowled. "Okay, whatever it was, why don't you go ahead and cough it out. It can't have been all that bad."

"It weren't very damn good," Bubba said. Sweat poured down his face. "I can't believe I was such an asshole but you know how a drunk is about his booze. When Anna got pissed off at Leroy, she grabbed hold of the whiskey bottle and started chug-a-luggin'. That's when I came back to the table and grabbed the bottle away from her. She got so mad she hauled off and smacked me one."

Bubba stopped and pulled a handkerchief out of his pocket to wipe his face. "You know I ain't the hittin' type—especially with women but it musta been a reflex 'cause when she did that, I hauled off and damn near knocked her outta her chair."

Kelly frowned and shook his head. "I can imagine Anna's reaction to that."

"Yeah! She grabbed the bottle and whacked it down on the table so hard it damn near broke bottle and table both. Then she kicked back her chair, grabbed her bag, told me and Leroy to kiss her ass and hightailed it for the door."

"So that was the last time you talked to her?"

"Yeah, but she made a couple of remarks before she got out the door you might want to ask Cam about.

"How's that?"

Bubba shrugged his shoulders. "I'd rather you asked Cam."

"Okay, I'm going to have a talk with him anyhow. Likely he'll bring it up himself."

"I still feel like shit," Bubba said.

"That won't do any good, Bubba." Kelly gave the little guy a straight, hard look. "You had no way of knowing Anna was going to be murdered. The way I see it, the two of you had a lot of good times together and I'm sure that's what she'd want you to remember."

Bubba lifted his head and tried a weak smile. "Thanks, Kelly. At least I feel better knowing you understand what happened last night."

Kelly smiled. "Not to worry," he said. "I know you were a good friend of Anna's."

Bubba slid out of the booth. "A few of us are getting together tonight to have a few drinks and kinda give Anna a sendoff," he said. "Think you could stop by?"

Kelly nodded. There'd be lots of loose talk flying around and that kind of get together was good for bringing out the gossip. He just might hear something interesting. "I'll be there," he said. "I think it's a good idea getting together to talk about old times. It'll make everybody feel better."

"Anna always said she wanted a big wake," Bubba said. Tears welled up in his eyes. "I best get over there and see if that bunch wants to come." He stuck out his hand and Kelly gave him a firm grip.

"You take it easy now," Kelly said.

Bubba nodded and headed toward the round table.

Kelly glanced across the room and saw Darlene had arrived while he was busy with Bubba. Cam looked up and nodded and Kelly crossed the room to join him behind the bar.

"We'll go out this way." Cam led Kelly through the kitchen, out the back door and across a grassy lot. Cam's private quarters were separated from the Hideaway by a hedge of tall evergreens. The two men approached a rustic bachelor's cabin. Cam opened the front door and they stepped into a small room dominated by a stone fireplace. Inside, Cam motioned Kelly to one of the leather chairs flanking the fireplace.

"I'll plug the coffee in," he said and crossed to a small efficiency kitchen. He plugged a pot into the wall and grabbed a beer from the refrigerator.

Kelly sank into the soft leather and stretched his legs.

"I think I've got myself in a jam," Cam said. He joined Kelly and settled into the other chair.

"How's that?"

"I had another argument with Anna after you left last night."

Kelly studied the other man's face. His friend was on the verge of exploding. Ten to one there was more to this than an argument egged on by booze. "From what I remember of Anna's condition, I'd be more surprised if you hadn't mixed it up with her again," Kelly said.

"There's things you don't know about me 'n Anna." A slow flush spread up Cam's neck. "I'm kinda sensitive about it but I suppose you heard I've been having some money trouble."

Kelly nodded. "I'd heard but there's no shame in that. Ever since the oil patches went dry, even the high rollers been under the gun."

"I know but this isn't the first time. A couple of years back, I damn near lost the place. I'd heard talk that Anna had some bucks, so I hit her up for a loan. She let me have it but she wasn't no fool. She had Bill Shipton write up the note. The way he worded it, she'd get the Hideaway if I defaulted on the payments."

"That's standard in one of those notes." Kelly frowned. He didn't like the direction things were going. Money and murder were a nasty combination. "Are you trying to say you'd gotten behind on the payments?"

Cam looked embarrassed. "At first, I paid her right on the dot but things got tight and I started to let them slide. She never raised a fuss and I guess I kinda took her for granted."

"Did you ever get her paid?"

"Almost. It's been a tough year though, and to tell you the truth, a couple of days ago I asked her if she could let me have another five thousand."

"Throwing her out of the bar probably wasn't too smart a move considering you were in default."

"I know. I was stupid. When I asked her for the money, she didn't even mention what I still owed her...just said she'd think about it. Then when she came in yesterday afternoon, I asked her again and she jumped all over me."

"Was she drunk or sober?"

The bar owner lit a cigarette, taking a deep drag before he answered. "She was cold sober but man, was she mean. I'd never seen Anna like that. She had me scared and that's the truth."

"Were Bubba and Leroy in the bar?"

"No, this was earlier."

"She came over to the bar before the flea market closed then?"

"Yeah. She stopped for a quick beer on her dinner break.

"So did the money question come up again later?"

"Not directly but she hinted about it when she started in on me for asking her to leave. I wouldn't have eighty-sixed her but she was getting so damn drunk I was afraid to let her stay."

Kelly nodded. "You'd have been in a real jam if the cops had shown up."

"Don't I know it." Cam rolled his eyes. "And Anna knew it too," he said. "This wasn't the first time I've had to throw her out. She's done it before but she never held a grudge and once she sobered up she always thanked me for seeing that she got home."

"She would," Kelly said.

"I should've known better last night though. Something was biting her hard and she was taking it out on everybody."

"Maybe she was having money problems and getting riled was an excuse to turn you down. Had she been acting like she was short of cash lately?"

"Hell, no. She hadn't been any different from normal 'til yesterday. Like I said, when I first asked her about the money, it didn't faze her a bit. All she said was that she'd think about it and get back to me."

"What happened after I left her with Bubba and Leroy?"

"Nothing at first. She ignored me. Then she started a ruckus with them. It got pretty loud and the next thing I knew, she grabbed her bag and kicked over the chair. I figured 'good, she's outta here, but I spoke too soon. She got as far as the front door. Then she stopped, blew up her cheeks and at the top of her lungs told the whole damn bar she was calling my note and taking over this place."

Kelly frowned. "That was probably the booze talking," he said. "You know Anna. She never meant half of what she said when she'd taken on a full load."

"Not this time," Cam said. "You shoulda seen the look on her face. Anyway, I wasn't about to let it slide. I grabbed my coat, tossed the till key at Darlene and took off after Anna."

"Was she going to her cabin?"

"Nope. She went straight down the hill toward the flea market. I tried to get her to stop but she was raving. The wind was blowing a gale and it was raining so hard I couldn't see two feet ahead. Anna fell down a couple of times and I tried to help her up but she shook me off and told me to keep my filthy hands to myself."

Kelly's eyebrows went up. "That must've been some sight."

Cam nodded. "I finally caught up with her on the bridge, then I had to wrestle her against a railing to get her stopped."

Kelly shook his head.

"I know. It looks bad and that's not the worst of it. She kept kicking and fighting. Then she bit my hand and I guess something snapped. I pinned her up against the railing and told her I'd wring her scrawny neck if she didn't shut her mouth."

"Not the best choice of words," Kelly said. "But since that scene was just between you and Anna, you'd probably be better off to forget it happened."

"I wish I could but Frank was down at the foot of the bridge putting up his boat. I know damn well he saw me shove Anna up against the railing and he probably heard what I said. My voice was pretty loud.

"I didn't spot Frank until after Anna took off. He was up against the piling, close enough to hear loud voices and you can bet your ass he was listening as hard as he could. There's not one chance in a million he'll keep his mouth shut either. You know Frank."

Kelly nodded agreement. "What was Frank doing down there at that time of night?"

"I don't know. He'd probably been out night fishing. He's out there every time the game warden's back is turned. The storm must've forced him off the lake."

"Well, it's too bad in one way but at least he'll be able to vouch for the fact you left Anna on the bridge and went back to the bar?"

Cam flinched. "That's part of the problem. After Anna took off for the flea market, I walked across the bridge and down to the pilings. I figured I'd wait out the storm and maybe have a few words with Frank. But when I got there, he'd disappeared. I hung around for about thirty minutes but there wasn't any sign of him. It must have been after one when I started back up the hill."

"That's not so good."

"No and what's worse, I didn't go right back to the bar."

"Why not?"

"I was still too shook up. I figured I needed some cooling off time so I went to the house. I didn't get back to the bar until closing time."

Kelly fastened his gaze on the fireplace and collected his thoughts.

"I won't kid you." He brought his eyes back to Cam. "Once the cops find out about that struggle on the bridge, they'll settle on you like ticks on a hound dog."

"Don't I know it." Cam drained off his beer and nursed the empty mug. "I swear to God, Kelly, I didn't have anything to do with Anna's murder. She was alive when I left her and I don't have a clue how she ended up dead inside the flea market."

"It's too bad you took so long getting back to the bar. That doesn't look good."

"I know what it looks like."

Kelly doubted Cam realized just how bad things were but he'd better get him as prepared as he could. "You were sure as hell in the wrong place at the wrong time last night. I know how Gus thinks and he'll look at the facts and you've just admitted opportunity, the whole bar heard Anna's threat about your note, so that takes care of the motive and since she was strangled with a silk scarf you could've picked up anywhere that takes care of means. Frankly, I'd be surprised if they didn't arrest you on the spot."

Cam groaned and gripped his head. "Maybe I ought to pack up and get the hell out of here for a while."

"That's the worst thing you could do." Kelly fixed Cam with a hard stare. "Do you want every cop in the state on your tail?"

Cam shook his head. "What do you think I should do?"

"I think you ought to call Bill Shipton and tell him the whole story. You're in deep shit no matter what but if you and Bill go see Gus and tell him exactly what happened last night, at least he'll know you're not trying to hide anything."

Cam stared at his glass. "If I do that, will you investigate Anna's death for me? Once I'm arrested, the cops won't look too hard for the real killer and I'm scared shitless I'm going to go down on a murder rap."

Kelly sighed. He'd been expecting this and deep down, he knew he wanted to get involved. "I'm willing to see what I can do but first I'll have to talk it over with Gus," he said. "It's his case and I can't go mucking around in a murder investigation without his okay. That's the best I can do for you."

Cam nodded and attempted a smile. "That's all I'm asking."

Kelly stood up and extended his hand. "Keep your chin up," he said. "Get hold of Bill and do what he says. If anybody can talk you out of jail, Bill's the man to do it. Matter of fact, Gus is liable to leave you loose just to shut him up."

Kelly chuckled, then choked it off. Cam's face had gone dead white at the mention of jail.

Chapter Four

Jack Boscon unfolded the morning edition of the *Fort Worth Star Telegram* and frowned at the headline.

"Wouldn't that be a kick in the teeth?" he growled and continued to read the story about a woman who'd been strangled at the Indian Creek flea market.

A security guard had discovered her body when he made late rounds. The victim's name was being withheld pending notification of next of kin and the police were asking the public's help in locating a young woman who had reportedly been involved in a dispute with the victim earlier in the day.

The paper gave a description of the young woman and Jack had a sinking feeling he knew who she was.

A couple of weeks before, a young woman named Krystal Davis had hired him to find her mother. According to her story, her father had shot himself seventeen years earlier and her mother had disappeared that same night. Krystal had spent her childhood with her grandmother and an uncle and neither of them would talk about her mother.

Jack had gotten the idea from the flat, emotionless tone she'd used when she talked about her family they hadn't lost much love on Krystal.

Krystal had explained that she'd inherited her father's controlling interest in Davis Oil and in three months, on her twenty-fifth birthday, she'd gain control of the trust that held the company's assets. In other words, she was fixing to become a very wealthy woman and she was determined to know the truth about her mother. She wanted her mother found and she also wanted a sketch of her mother's lifestyle.

Jack had warned Krystal that if her mother wanted to stay lost, she'd be covered deep and the investigation would likely be expensive. She'd shrugged off the expense and asked him to start immediately.

Jack had done some surveillance work for Krystal's uncle Andrew Davis a few years back, so he was familiar with the family but he'd never handled any of their personal business and he figured it wouldn't hurt to be on the good side of the young heiress.

He'd started Krystal's job the next morning. He hadn't expected much on the first run-through, but he'd plugged Anna Davis' name into the computer and was surprised to come up with six possible matches. Within hours he'd finished the cross-matching and had a make. Anna hadn't even tried to hide. She had a flea market license from Tarrant County that gave her place of residence as Indian Creek, a small community on the outskirts of Fort Worth.

The next morning Jack cruised out to Indian Creek where a young fellow at the gas station asked if he was a fisherman. Jack nodded and said he'd heard Indian Creek was a good spot for fishing. The kid assured him it was hot. Jack thanked the gas jockey. Then he hung a camera around his neck and went in search of the locals, posing as a writer for *Field and* Stream.

His first stop was the flea market, where he snapped a few random pictures and asked a talkative old geezer where he might find Anna Davis. Jack did some reconnoitering and managed to snap a couple of pictures while Anna waited on customers.

He finished at the flea market and went in search of gossip. He'd spotted the Hideaway on his way in and figured that as the likeliest spot for gossip. He made it his next stop.

Inside, a group of old timers were gathered around a potbellied stove. Jack sat for a while at the bar, then ordered a round and introduced himself. It hadn't taken Jack long to spot Frank Perkins as the blabbermouth of the bunch and with a little manipulating, he'd managed to hire Frank and his boat for a tour around the lake.

The investment had been more than profitable. Jack gleaned a wealth of information from the old man, who seemed to know everything about everyone. When Jack casually brought Anna Davis' name into the conversation as a woman he'd met at the flea market and tried to interview, Frank let out a snort.

"I'm surprised she didn't take a shotgun to you. She probably hadn't hit the whiskey yet."

"Likes the sauce, does she? Drowning old sorrows or what?"

Frank shrugged. "Hell, nobody knows about her. She's been around this Creek for more'n fifteen years but she hasn't ever had a visitor I know of. She wasn't a bad-looking woman when she first showed up here but she turned herself into a hag in a hell of a hurry. Most of us figure she was married to some rich dude and when she started hitting the bottle, he paid her to get the hell out of his life."

"Could be an interesting story but I don't think I'd like to get myself shot trying to dig into it."

"I'd forget her if I was you. I doubt if there's much to it other than what I said. One thing though. She's got a pile of dough hid somewhere around the Creek."

"How do you know that?"

"Well, I can't rightly say how I know." Frank smirked and looked pleased with himself. "You can take my word for it, though. She's stashed a pile somewhere. I know that for a fact."

Jack recognized cagey when he heard it but he hadn't been hired to dig into Anna's finances, so he'd shrugged it off. Krystal's instructions called for him to find her mother and get a rundown on her lifestyle. With more than enough to wrap up the job, Jack left Indian Creek that night.

The next day he'd left a message on Krystal's answering machine.

She'd appeared in his office a couple of hours later, breathless and trembling. "I want to hear it in person."

Jack chuckled and motioned her to a seat. "I'm glad I've got something to report." He'd smiled and tapped a manila folder.

"Do you mean you've found her already?"

"Yep, sure have. Sometimes I just get lucky and this was one of those times." Handing her the folder, he'd expected her to open it immediately but she'd just sat there clutching it to her chest.

"Aren't you going to look?"

She bite her lip but finally nodded, opened the cover and spread it out on the desk. Clipped to the inside was a photograph of a haggard and emaciated woman. Wisps of gray hair clung to her head and her deep brown eyes had a haunted expression.

"Oh!" Krystal gasped. "She looks so old."

Jack leaned back and closed his eyes. Poor kid. If she thought the picture was bad, wait 'til she read the report. When he opened his eyes again she was staring at the photograph.

"You still want to meet her?"

She'd blinked a couple of times, then nodded her head.

"Okay. It's your call but if I can make a suggestion, why don't you go down to that flea market on Saturday when she's working her stall? As you'll see from the report, she drinks a bit and she's more likely to be sober then. I think that might be better, don't you?"

Krystal looked like she was fighting back tears. Jack patted her hand. She blinked a couple of times and finally answered. "Yes. Thanks. I don't know what I'm going to say but I've got to see her."

That had been three days ago. Now this. He glared at the newspaper and felt a little sick to his stomach. It wouldn't do business any good if it got out that he'd set the girl up to murder her mother.

Sighing, he grabbed his keys and headed out the door. Frank Perkins was sure to know what was going on out there and Jack wanted confirmation the body was Anna's before he took any steps.

When he passed the Hideaway, Jack saw the lot was already full of vehicles. No doubt murder was the main attraction but he kept on down the hill toward Frank's cabin. He'd just as soon keep this visit as quiet as possible.

Frank wasn't home but Jack walked down to the creek and spotted him at the dock.

"Hi." He strolled up to Frank and lifted a hand. "You remember me?"

Frank, who'd been bending over the boat, stood up and squinted. "Sure," he said. "I remember. You get the assignment for that boating story?"

"I'm still waiting to hear from the editor. I see you've had a bit of excitement. Surprised the hell out of me when I read the paper. They didn't give the name of the woman who was murdered though. Anybody I know?"

"It was Anna Davis that got it. You remember me telling you there was some fishy stuff going on with her? Well, she sure as hell got on the wrong side of somebody."

"You called that one, all right." Jack smiled and put plenty of syrup in his voice. "Frank, do the cops have a line on the killer?"

"Well, there's some speculation about that." Frank puffed out his chest. "'Fraid I can't go into detail," he said. "They've asked me to give them a hand, you know."

Frank reminded Jack of a bantam rooster. "It's a bit of luck for them—you being on the spot." Jack said, being careful to keep a straight face. "I hope you'll keep me in mind, if anything breaks down here."

"You thinking about doing a story?" Frank's eyes lit up as he contemplated his part in a local whodunit.

"I'm considering it," Jack said. "Of course, I'd need a fresh approach. That's where I thought you might help. What about the money angle? Didn't you mention something about buried treasure?"

"Aw, there's nothing in that." Frank lowered his head and scuffed the dirt with his boot. "You know how guys get together and bullshit. Don't mean nothin'."

"I see," Jack said.

Frank turned his head and nodded toward the bait house. "There's a couple of fishermen waiting for me," he said. "I gotta get goin'."

Jack'd already gotten what he needed. "Nice seein' you again, Frank," he said. "I'd appreciate a call if you come across anything I can use."

On the way back to Fort Worth, he mulled over their conversation. Frank had done some fancy backpedaling on that story he'd told about Anna having money hidden away. The little weasel was probably hoping to find her stash and keep it for himself.

Sighing, Jack pushed Frank to the back of his mind. He'd best swing by Krystal's apartment. At least he could give her a warning before he went to the cops.

Krystal was a graduate student at Texas Christian University and lived in one of the off-campus apartments on Camp Bowie Boulevard. It was only a short run across town.

The Mexican-style complex was attractive, neat, well landscaped and carefully tended. Jack knocked on the door of 103, waited, then rapped again, harder. Finally, the handle turned and the door opened the length of a chain. An Asian girl peered through the crack.

"Yes?" She aimed her eyes at his feet.

"I'd like to see Krystal Davis."

"Why?"

"It's kind of important. If you'll tell her it's Jack Boscon, I think she'll want to see me."

"Mr. Boscon. Krissie's detective?" She released the chain and opened the door.

Jack suppressed a grin. During his stint in Vietnam, he'd learned enough about Asian custom to know eye contact was considered rude. She still hadn't looked at his face. He stepped inside and followed her into a tiny kitchenette. A round glass table, set with a tea pot and cups, faced the window. A cereal bowl filled with a milky rice mixture showed he'd caught her in the midst of breakfast.

"You like tea? Krissie having a shower. You wait?"

"Thanks." Jack pulled out a chair. "I'm not much of a tea drinker."

She darted a glance at his chin and nodded. "Krissie laughs at tea. No drink."

"I'm afraid you have the advantage of me," he said. "I don't know your name."

"It's Kwon. Ah…Penny Kwon."

She was obviously still struggling with English. In Chinese, the surname came first. "Nice to meet you, Penny. You're not from around these parts?"

"No. Guangzhou. Canton. You know Hong Kong? Near there."

"That must be quite a change for you. Canton to Texas."

She lifted her eyes, made contact and dropped her head. "Yes."

"How did you happen to hook up with Krystal? She's from Houston, isn't she?"

"Krissie rent this apartment when she first come here to school. I am exchange student. Krissie have ad in school paper. We like each other. Mr. Boscon, I ask something?"

"Jack."

"Jack." She nodded. "I worry for Krissie. You bring bad news, yes?"

Jack frowned. "Why do you ask?"

She fidgeted, her fingers twisting a paper napkin. "Krissie like sister. She upset about mother. Meeting go very bad."

So, she did go out to the flea market. Jack's heart sank at hearing the confirmation that the mysterious woman had indeed been Krystal. "Did anything happen out there?" he asked.

Penny tensed and her face paled. She shrunk back in her chair and tightened her lips.

Jack pressed on. "Can you tell me exactly what time Krystal got home last night?"

Penny's fingers shredded the napkin and she glanced at the doorway. "Shower stop. Krissie here soon."

"It's important, Penny. I need to make sure she was home before midnight."

Relief flooded Penny's face. She bobbed her head. "Krissie home early. Clock say only seven."

"Did she stay in all night or did she maybe go out again?"

"No. She take pills for sleep. Go to bed."

Jack frowned. "You're sure?"

"Very small apartment." Penny waved her arm in a circle. "Krissie no leave. Sleep all night."

"Okay. I hate to break it to you like this but Krystal's mother was murdered last night."

Penny clapped her hand to her mouth.

"Apparently it happened sometime between midnight and two a.m., so you're going to be an important witness for Krystal."

"Witness! Witness? Explain."

"The police will want you to tell them what you've just told me."

Shaking her head back and forth, she clutched her arms across her breasts. "Police? No police. I no talk police."

"Don't be scared." Jack smiled to reassure her. "It's different here. Talking to the police is nothing. They'll ask you a lot of questions but as long as you tell them the truth, they'll treat you just fine."

Her voice rose. "No. Must be other way."

"Tell me about yesterday afternoon?" Jack changed the subject.

"I wait. Krissie tell you." Penny kept her head down but Jack spotted tears through her fingers.

"If Krystal was as upset as you say, she might not remember." Jack's voice was gentle, encouraging. "If I know the whole story, I'll be able to help when the police question you."

Penny lifted her head and almost met his eyes. "Krissie go to Houston. Come home. Say she hire detective to find mother." Penny paused and glanced at the doorway.

Jack took a sip of coffee, waited a moment then nodded encouragement. Finally, Penny continued. "Krissie not talk much. She have fight with uncle. She ask him tell her about mother and father. He no tell. Krissie angry."

"Did Krystal tell her uncle she was going to hire someone to find her mother?"

"Not say." Penny shrugged.

"Okay, that's fine." Jack said. "Now, what about yesterday afternoon. Did Krystal say how she planned to approach her mother?"

"No."

"Do you know what caused the ruckus?"

A puzzled expression crossed her face and she tilted her head. "Ruckus? I not know this."

"Sorry. I mean, what happened that made the security guard think Krystal was attacking her mother?"

"Man come with whiskey. Mother drink. Krissie no like that. She try grab bottle, trip and fall into mother."

"Did Krissie strike her?"

"Not hit. Fall over chair. Guard person come. Krissie run away."

Jack shook his head. "I was afraid something might happen out there. Anna wasn't exactly Harriet Nelson."

Penny's face clouded again and Jack corrected himself. "Sorry, that was an inside joke about an old television shows I'm sure you've never seen."

"Very bad thing. Krissie not like to talk."

"I'll go easy on her. She'll have to be told about her mother's death, though, and she'll need to explain to the police."

"I go get Krissie now? You like music?"

Jack nodded and gave her a friendly smile. She reached across the table and turned on the radio. Another Asian custom—entertain your guests.

"Thanks," he said. "You go get Krystal. I'll be fine."

She padded out of the room. Jack leaned back and listened to a country ballad. Sunlight streamed in the window and whoops of laugher drifted up from the swimming pool. After Penny'd been gone about five minutes, Jack started to get restless. He was up, pacing the floor, when a news bulletin caught his attention.

"Early this morning the body of a white, middle-aged woman was found by a security guard at the Indian Creek flea market. The woman, whose name is being withheld pending notification of next of kin, had been strangled. The coroner estimates time of death between eleven-thirty p.m. and one-thirty a.m.

"Police are seeking a young woman who was involved in a struggle with the deceased earlier in the day. This woman is in her early twenties, attractive, with light blond hair and a slim figure. She is approximately five feet five or six and was wearing dark wool slacks and a red-and-blue print sweater. Police are asking anyone with information to contact the Tarrant County Sheriff's Department."

Jack heard a gasp and jerked his head around. Krystal stood in the doorway. She had her hair pulled back and tied with a scarf and her slim body was wrapped in an oversize white robe. All the blood drained from her face, leaving it the color of chalk. Just as she slumped, Penny—who barely reached five feet—grabbed her from behind.

"I've got her," Jack said

Penny nodded and allowed Jack to lift Krystal into his arms.

"This way." She led him into a small living room.

Jack settled Krystal onto the couch and stood back. Penny dropped to her knees, smoothed Krystal's hair and crooned reassurances.

The lyrics of a Texas line dance pulsed from the radio. Jack walked back to the kitchen and shut it off. Silence gripped the room. Tears spilled down Krystal's cheeks and Penny fetched a washcloth to wipe her friend's eyes.

"I never even got to ask my mother why Daddy killed himself," Krystal sobbed.

"It's okay, Krissie," Penny soothed.

Krystal lay silent for several moments, then opened her eyes and focused her gaze on Jack.

"Is this why you're here?" she asked in a barely audible voice.

Jack bent down beside the couch and took her hand. "It was in the morning paper. I'm afraid I'm going to have to talk to the police but I wanted to give you some time to prepare yourself for their questions."

"Oh, no!" Her eyes sprang open. "I can't see the police. I've got to talk to Uncle Andrew first. He doesn't even know I hired you to find my mother. I've got to go to Houston. I can't tell him on the telephone. I just can't."

Jack frowned and shook his head. "I'm afraid I can't wait that long. I could lose my license for withholding information in a murder case."

Krystal clutched his hand, her eyes wide and pleading. "Couldn't you wait a couple of hours? Please. Just give me time to catch a plane to Houston and tell my uncle in person."

Her voice was pathetic. Damn! He always went soft when a pretty young thing begged for help. "I'm taking a big chance here but I guess I can give you that much. I have some business over in Arlington that'll take me 'til about four. I'll head over there now and call in at the cop shop after I'm done."

"Thank you." She smiled through her tears.

"I call. Get seat on plane." Penny said. She lifted her eyes to Jack and gave him a warm, grateful smile.

Jack let himself out of the apartment and walked back to his pickup.

Jack leaned against his truck and took a deep breath. It'd seemed like a good idea back when Krystal hired him to confirm things with her Uncle Andrew. Andrew'd sure thought so and been grateful for Jack's confidence. He'd felt a bit guilty at the time. Technically it was a violation of Krystal's confidence. But given the circumstances, he'd eased his own conscience by reassuring himself that it was in Krystal's best interests to keep her uncle informed. The money Andrew paid him for duplicate copies of his reports hadn't hurt any, either.

What the hell! It was a tough business and a man had to look out for himself if he wanted to stay independent. Jack gave himself a mental shake and climbed into his truck.

"I'll give her a break and then wash my hands of it," he muttered. He turned the key and started the truck.

By the time he'd pulled out onto Camp Bowie, his mind was fixed on his client in Arlington and Krystal's problems were left behind.

Chapter Five

"I'll be just fine." Krystal leaned across the seat and gave Penny a hug.

She unlocked the car door and pulled the handle, then turned back to Penny. "Now I don't want you to worry anymore. I'm going to talk to Uncle Andrew and he'll take care of everything."

"You will telephone?"

"I'll call as soon as I talk to Uncle Andrew. That's a promise."

Krystal hopped out of the car and headed to the terminal. At the Southwest Airlines booth, she stepped up to the counter and smiled at the ticket agent.

"May I help you?" His voice was crisp and professional but his eyes brightened at the sight of the stunning blonde holding out her American Express card and his smile held real warmth.

"I have a reservation for the noon flight to Houston." Krystal returned his smile with an automatic twist of her lips.

She sighed with relief when she boarded and found the plane almost empty. She couldn't have handled a talkative seat companion. She needed quiet time to get her thoughts in order.

After take-off, Krystal leaned back in the seat and turned her face to the window. Memory rolled in with the passing clouds, taking her back, back in time, to the Saturday before her seventh birthday. Mommy had promised her a big party with clowns. She'd gone to sleep dreaming about the clowns. Then she'd heard a loud bang.

"Mommy!"

Mommy didn't come. She'd buried her head under the covers and cried.

"Would you care for a soft drink?" A friendly voice brought Krystal back from the past.

"Thank you, no." She shook her head and the flight attendant crossed to the next seat across the aisle.

Turning back to the window, Krystal forced her thoughts away from the past, to how to handle Uncle Andrew. The last time she'd been home, they'd had a fight over her mother, a fight she remembered word for word.

"I'll be twenty-five in a couple of months. Don't you think it's time somebody told me the truth about my mother?"

"She wasn't a fit woman to raise a child!

"At least you could tell me why she left!"

"No, as a matter of fact, I couldn't. I have no idea what was in her mind. She had no interest in you when you were a child and there's no reason to think that's changed. You'll only rake open old sores if you try to find her."

"Do you know where she went when she left Houston?"

"I have no idea where she went and furthermore, I don't care. Nor do I want to carry this discussion any further."

Krystal slammed out of the study and spent the rest of the night in her bedroom. She'd had her own agenda though and Saturday morning, as soon as they'd both left—Stella for the beauty parlor and Uncle Andrew for golf—she'd gone to the attic and spent hours digging through old trunks and unpacking stacks of photo albums. She'd made up her mind to hire a detective. He'd need a picture, and there had to be one here somewhere. Except there wasn't. Finally, tired and sweaty, she'd pushed the last trunk back into place and started to leave. Then she'd spotted a small leather suitcase tucked away in an alcove.

It'd taken a while but she'd jimmied the lock and opened the case. More linen. Disgusted, she'd lifted a handful. A faded pink jewelry folder lay on a stack of doilies. She'd picked it up and it crinkled in her hands. Untying the satin ribbon, she'd pulled out a long white envelope. The writing, scrawled in her grandmother's spidery hand, had been impossible to read without her glasses. She'd tucked the envelope into her pocket, closed the suitcase and stacked it back in the alcove.

"The captain has turned on the seatbelt sign." The flight attendant's voice brought Krystal back to the present and the descent into Houston.

After she deplaned and rushed through the terminal, she strode toward the long line of taxis waiting in front of the airport. She jumped into the first in line and gave the driver her uncle's address in River Oaks. Then she settled back in the seat and tried to concentrate on her upcoming talk with Uncle Andrew. It was hopeless. Her mind kept darting between the past and the present. When the cab swung into the drive, she still hadn't figured out what to say.

The cab dropped her off at the front entrance. Krystal peeked through the garage window. The Jaguar was gone so Stella was off somewhere but the BMW was there. Thank God. Uncle Andrew'd probably be up in his study. She let herself in and climbed the stairs to the second floor. She walked noiselessly down the hall to the big corner room and knocked on the door.

"What is it?" Andrew grumbled.

Krystal turned the knob and stepped inside the room. Uncle Andrew, a small, neat man with dark, gray-streaked hair, lifted his head. His sharp brown eyes on Krystal's face.

"I didn't know you were coming home this weekend," he said.

"I wasn't. Something's happened and I need to talk to you."

"You'd better sit down." He motioned to a chair in front of his desk. "What's happened?"

Krystal sat and met his unblinking gaze. He never relaxed. His dress, like his manner, was always rigid and proper. She took a deep breath.

"I hired a detective agency to find my mother."

Andrew's face tightened. "I thought we went all through this business of Anna the last time you were here."

Krystal's eyes flashed. "What you mean is that I begged you to tell me about my mother and father and you refused. What did you expect me to do?"

He shook his head. His eyelids drooped and hid his expression. "Did you get your answers?"

She hesitated, then shook her head.

"I'm sorry." A sigh escaped his lips. "I was only trying to spare you."

Krystal gripped her lip with her teeth. She wanted to scream at him but her courage wavered. She dropped her eyes and covered her face with her hands.

"You know your Aunt Stella and I have your best interests at heart?"

Krystal shook her head. "Maybe you care but don't try and tell me Stella gives a damn, because I won't believe it."

"Okay." He ignored the dig at Stella. "Let's not quarrel. Why don't you tell me what happened?" Andrew leaned back in his chair, his fingers steepled under his chin.

"I went to see my mother. And made a complete fool of myself."

Andrew frowned. "Go on."

"I fell into her and knocked her out of her chair. It was nothing, really but it looked bad. A security guard came and pulled me off her."

"Then you haven't talked to Anna yet?"

Krystal shook her head. "No. And I'll never get another chance because somebody went to the flea market last night and killed her."

"What?" Andrew jerked forward.

"She's dead. The detective told me about it this morning. They found her body out at the flea market and they're looking for me."

"Why would they be looking for you?" He kept his eyes on her face.

"Because somebody told them I attacked her." Krystal's voice trembled and she fought back tears. "I wasn't there last night, if that's what you're wondering. I didn't want her dead. I wanted her alive so I could talk to her. Now the police are looking for me and it's all your fault. If you'd answered my questions, I wouldn't have hired a detective. I know you don't want any more scandal in the family but what am I supposed to do now?"

"Please, Krystal." His voice was almost gentle. "I was wrong. I admit it. I didn't realize you were so desperate you'd go to a detective. If it's so important to you we can talk about it later. Right now we need to decide what to do. You say you haven't talked to the police yet?"

"No. As soon as I heard about it, I had Penny drive me to the airport."

"Good. I'll get Tom Masters and have him call Fort Worth. This business is best handled by a lawyer. Tom can explain and try to put some pressure on the police to keep your name out of the papers. Now. Where were you last night?"

"I was home in bed. I felt like a fool for losing control of myself at the flea market. I didn't feel like talking to anyone, not even Penny. I took a couple of sleeping pills and they knocked me out."

"Will Penny vouch for that?"

"Of course she will. Her bedroom's right next to mine. She knows I didn't go anywhere."

"Okay, that's good. Now why don't you go down to the kitchen and make us some sandwiches while I call Tom and get that over with."

When the door closed behind Krystal, Andrew reached for the telephone. "Hell of a mess," he muttered as he dialed his lawyer's private number. "Hi, Tom. Andrew Davis here. With a problem."

"What's so urgent it can't wait until Monday?" Tom sounded like he'd been roused from a nap.

"Anna's dead. She's been murdered."

"The hell you say! When did this happen?"

"Last night. Krystal says she was strangled."

"Krystal? She's not mixed up in this, is she?"

"She says not but the cops are looking for her."

"What for? Where is she?"

"Here with me. She says she didn't do anything."

"There must be some reason they're looking for her."

"She went out to Anna's flea market on Saturday afternoon and made a scene."

"What kind of a scene?"

"I don't know. She came in here with some wild story about falling and knocking Anna off her chair."

"Are you saying she was there when Anna was murdered?"

"No. That happened sometime in the middle of the night. Krystal left after the fracas with Anna. She claims she was home all night and her roommate will back her up."

"Good. That makes it easier. I'll call Fort Worth and find out who's on the case. Krystal will have to give them a statement but they won't be too hard on her. Now what about you? Are you clean?"

Andrew hesitated. When he spoke, his voice was strained. "That's the hitch. I took a run down there Saturday night. I wasn't all that sure Anna would keep her mouth shut and I wanted to have a talk with her."

"I told you on Friday to stay away from Anna!"

"Sure, that's easy for you to say but you know what my position is. All I wanted to do was find out where Anna stood. Frankly, if it seemed like she needed any encouragement, I was prepared to offer an increase in her annual income."

"That wasn't very smart. You should have left it in my hands."

"It's too late to worry about that now," Andrew said. "What's important is what to do about Krystal."

"Of course, you're right." Tom sighed. "You caught me at a bad moment. First things first. I assume you didn't kill her."

"Of course I didn't kill her! I didn't even see her. It was after ten when I got there and the place was dark. Krystal's detective had told me where Anna's cabin was but she wasn't home. I decided to hang around and wait. I pulled into a little day park they've got for the fishermen, where I could watch her front door. I waited 'til midnight but she never showed. I finally gave up and headed back home. I drove damn near all night and I'd just as soon not admit I'd been anywhere near there."

"Did anybody see you?"

"I don't think so. Like I said, it was dark and I was pretty well hidden. There was some old guy wandering around down at the boat house but I don't think he spotted me."

"You're sure that's everything?"

"Yes, I'm sure. Why?"

"Because if you know anything that might give the police a lead to Anna's murderer you need to talk to them."

"Well, I don't. Krystal said she was killed in the flea market and I never went near the place.

Listen, Tom, what I've told you is privileged information—for your ears only. I don't want anything to do with this mess and I have no intention of admitting I was at Indian Creek."

"Okay. Just keep in mind it's not impossible for the cops to learn you were out there. Now about Krystal. I'll call the county and make arrangements for them to take her statement. If, as you say, she was home in bed, they'll keep it pretty informal," the lawyer said. "I suggest you send her back to Fort Worth. I'll make arrangements for the detective in charge of the case to stop by and see her tomorrow."

"Maybe you ought to be there when they talk to her."

"Not if it's as cut-and-dried as you say. Have another talk with her. If what you've told me is the whole story, it'll be better if she gives them an informal statement. Cops get suspicious when you call a lawyer in just to answer a few simple questions. There's no use riling them if it isn't necessary. But tell Krystal if she gets the least bit uncomfortable with their questions to clam up and call me. I'll make sure I'm available and if there's a need, I'll catch a plane."

"Okay. Now, what about Anna's body? Something will have to be done there and I want it kept as quiet as possible."

"I'll take care of that, too. I assume you want her cremated. For Krystal's sake, you might want to put her ashes in the plot with Clayton. I'll let you talk to her about that. For now, let's get it over with and hope the newspaper boys don't make the connection."

After he hung up, Andrew sank back in his chair and stared at the wall. He hadn't lied to Tom. He just hadn't told him about the traffic ticket he'd gotten out on Boat Club Road.

"Damn!" He stood up and crossed to the window. Maybe he should have come clean with Tom. He didn't like the possibility of that ticket popping up and biting him in the ass. Still, the connection wasn't likely. Better to keep his mouth shut and hope for the best.

"Here's your sandwich." Krystal pushed open the door and approached his desk with a tray.

"Thanks." He took a plate and settled back in his chair. "I've got everything set in Fort Worth. Tom's going to call the detective on the case and explain your connection with Anna. They'll want to talk to you but it'll just be a formality."

"Thank you." Krystal smiled a ghost of a smile. "I'm sorry for what I said. I guess I was still a bit crazy after hearing about my mother."

"That's understandable." Andrew returned her smile, his voice was surprisingly gentle.

"You look worn out," he said. "Why don't you take yourself off to bed for a while?"

"Thanks. I am tired." Krystal stopped at his desk. "I'd still like to have that talk though," she said. "After all this is over."

Chapter Six

Kelly walked down the hill toward the bait house. The parking lot was jammed bumper-to-bumper with cars, trucks and motorcycles. Loud country music rocked out the open front door and a haze of smoke drifted toward the creek.

The ramshackle old store front where Bubba sold fish bait, tackle and cold drinks—especially beer—was lit up like a Texas chicken ranch. Kelly didn't get why the old dump was so popular. There wasn't a damn thing attractive about it. The decor was barn-board, trimmed with tarpaper. Worm boxes and minnow tanks cluttered the cement floor and the place reeked to high heaven.

None of that seemed to matter, though. Bubba's mismatched stools and chairs were always occupied. Fishermen came in, ordered a bucket of bait, parked themselves at the slab of plywood perched on two oil barrels that served as a table and passed the time swapping yarns and slurping brews from the well-stocked cooler.

It was after seven when Kelly stepped inside. The smell of bait, fish, shrimp and beer clogged his nostrils and he had to squint to see through the smoke.

"Hey, here's Kelly!" Doug Phillips hollered from the plywood table where eight or nine old timers clustered around a keg of beer. "He's the one found Anna's body."

Kelly strode over to the group, nodded and pulled out a chair.

"You got any ideas about what happened down there?" Brian Sanders filled a mug and handed it over to Kelly.

"Thanks." Kelly accepted the foaming mug. "I don't know what happened, Brian. It looks like someone snuck up behind Anna, knocked her down, then wrapped a scarf around her neck and choked her."

"Poor Anna." Brian reached for another mug. "She had a sharp tongue but she didn't deserve that."

"A few of the boys have been talking about last night," Doug broke in. "It seems Anna and Cam got into a shouting match along about midnight and Cam threw her outta the bar."

Kelly tilted back in his chair and studied the faces at the table. "And your point is?"

"No point." Doug avoided Kelly's eye. "We was just jawin'. 'Course, you know Cam followed her outta the bar."

Kelly shrugged. "Cam told me they'd had a few words. But right after that, Anna said she was going down to the flea market and get her money box. He doesn't know what happened after she left him on the bridge."

"So he says." Doug's face registered disbelief. "Kind of funny him not getting back to the bar until closing time."

"Seems to me you've had your own troubles with Anna, haven't you, Doug?"

"Hey, I didn't mean nothin'. None of us figgers Cam snuffed her. We was just curious, that's all."

"Well, you know what they say about curiosity."

Doug dropped his eyes.

Kelly looked around the table. "What I'd appreciate is having all of you think back and try to remember if you saw any strangers hanging around here yesterday."

"I did." Marty Jenkins had been sticking close to the beer keg. He walked over and joined the group. "I don't know if it means anything but did you see the blonde that drove up in the Mercedes convertible yesterday afternoon?"

"I've already mentioned her to the police," Kelly said, "but she left long before the market closed. Why? You got any idea who she was?"

"Nope." Marty pulled out a chair and joined the table. "That car she was drivin' was sure a honey, though. It was one of them silver-gray convertibles. Brand new, I'd say."

"Did you happen to get the license number?"

"Never thought to look." Marty shook his head. "You ain't gonna go shootin' off your mouth I said anythin', are you? I never paid no attention to that gal. It was the car what caught my eye. Ain't no way I want nuthin' to do with the cops. First thing you know they'll be figgering I'm the one that murdered Anna."

Kelly shrugged. "They might consider that withholding information."

Marty shook his head again. "It ain't up to me to talk to the damn cops just 'cause I happened to admire a good-lookin' car."

A commotion broke out across the room. Kelly stood up and peered through the smoke to see what was going on. A circle of men surrounded Bubba, who was standing nose-to-nose with Frank Perkins and shaking with anger.

"What's up?" Kelly walked over and stepped inside the circle.

"Aw, Bubba's just touchy." Frank sidled over to Kelly's side. "I didn't mean no harm. I was just askin' him about his fish camp. He's been braggin' for months he and Anna were goin' down to Florida to buy one.

"Just yesterday I heard Anna tell him he could shove that fish camp up his ass, then she goes and gets herself murdered. It kinda got me to wonderin'."

"You son of a bitch," Bubba growled. "She was just lettin' off steam 'cause she was pissed about something. Everybody around here's got your number, Frank. You're just tryin' to start some shit. You'd gut your own mother given half a chance."

"Don't mind him." Kelly took Bubba's arm and eased him away from the circle. "You know Frank," he said. "His own life's such a pile of crap stirring up other folks is all that keeps him going."

"Yeah, I know but Anna and me was gonna buy us a fish camp." Bubba turned his head and glared back at the group of men clustered around Frank. "She was just blowin' smoke when she told me to shove it."

"Don't worry about it," Kelly said. "You don't owe anybody an explanation."

"I keep thinkin' I oughta paid more attention to what was rilin' Anna. Something was sure enough stuck in her craw last night and if I'd asked, she mighta told me. Now it's too late. On top of everything, I don't need that asshole reminding me I'll probably never get my fish camp now."

"There's no use kicking yourself over what you might've done," Kelly said. "Don't let Frank get you down. We all know what he's like."

"Thanks, Kelly. I'll be all right." Bubba tried to smile. "I think I'll grab a beer and cool off for a bit."

As soon as Bubba left, Frank, his fat face glistening with sweat, moved over to stand beside Kelly. "I heard some stuff up on the bridge last night," he said.

"And just what did you hear, Frank?"

"'Fraid I can't say. I had to tell the cops, though and they told me to keep it under my hat. I know you used to be a cop but you ain't on the force now, are you?"

Frank reminded Kelly of Humpty Dumpty with his short fat body and dainty little hands that looked like they belonged in white gloves. Now, waiting for Kelly's response, his black eyes glittered. Kelly itched to slap his face but that was stupid. The jerk was trying to goad him. Kelly just shrugged.

"Then I guess you'd better keep your mouth shut. I reckon that'll be a challenge for you."

Frank blinked and deflated.

Disgusted, Kelly walked away. He'd had all he could take for one day. It was time to pack it in for the night. He ignored Frank, called goodnight to Bubba, waved to the group at the table and headed out the door.

The short walk in the cold night air cleared some of the smoke out of Kelly's lungs. It'd been one hell of a long day and night and he was bone tired. When he reached the cabin and opened the door, Jake stood up and wagged a welcome.

"Looks like things have quieted down around here," Kelly slipped off his jacket and bent down to give the dog a body rub. He let Jake outside and spotted the red light blinking on his answering machine when he turned back from the door.

"Got your message, Kelly," Gus' voice boomed in his ear. "Angelo's sounds like a winner. I've got a bit of news to pass along but it'll keep 'til then. I should make it by six but if you get there first, grab a table and order me the large mixed rack. See you then."

Kelly let Jake back in and the two of them headed toward the bedroom.

"You know, Jake, it wouldn't surprise me if Gus has already found out who that woman is."

Jake flopped down on the rug beside the bed and settled his nose between his paws.

"You're right, boy. Past time to hit the hay. I'm right behind you."

Sunlight streamed through the window when Kelly opened his eyes again. He checked his bedside clock. It was eight—two hours past his usual hour for rising—but the flea market was closed, so other than a quick pass of the outbuildings, his time was his own.

Kelly took a shower and made a pot of coffee, then grabbed a notebook and settled down at the kitchen table. Years ago his criminology professor had stressed the importance of getting your facts in order before starting an investigation. Right now, Kelly needed some organization.

He started a timetable, jotting down the names of everybody who'd been in the vicinity of the flea market between midnight and two a.m. Then he tried thinking of a motive for everybody on his list. He started with Cam, who owed her money. Frank's name was next and after staring at the paper for a bit, he settled for cussedness.

By the time Kelly got to Leroy and Marty's names, he'd decided the list was a dumb idea but he was determined to finish. After several minutes of gnawing the end of his pencil, he finally skipped their names and moved on to Bubba. The bait-man could have had a couple of motives. Kelly wrote them down. Fish-camp, lover's quarrel. Then he stopped, read back over what he'd written and shook his head. This wasn't getting him anywhere.

He grabbed his jacket and headed for the door. "Take care of the place," he told Jake. "I'm going to have another talk with Bubba."

Maybe Bubba'd seen something he hadn't thought to mention. Though with the whiskey he'd drunk, he probably wouldn't remember a Mack truck roaring through the bar. Worth a try, though. If nothing else, Kelly could find out what time Bubba and Leroy left the bar.

Bubba was running around filling bait cans and handing out tackle to a group of fishermen. Kelly caught his attention, nodded toward the picnic table to indicate he wanted a chat, then grabbed a cola from the machine and settled down to wait.

September was winding down and an early frost had dappled the creek with signs of fall. The leaves on the poplar trees were tinged yellow and the marsh grasses were more gold than green. There was a nip in the air, even with the sun shining and Kelly had his windbreaker zipped.

Sitting there, watching ripples lap against the creek bank, Kelly's thoughts drifted back on his time at Indian Creek. Five years ago when he'd come here he'd been seeking a place to hide and heal his wounds. He hadn't planned to stay more than a year or two but time had passed and now he couldn't imagine any other way of life.

Lynda would've loved it down here. She'd always wanted them to move into a little house in the country where they could have a fenced yard and a couple of kids running around. Kelly had called it her picket fence syndrome. If only he'd taken her seriously and moved her out of the city before that awful night when the bikers, armed with whiskey bottles rigged into Molotov cocktails, had started the fire that took her life.

"Hey, what's up?" Bubba's voice broke through Kelly's dark thoughts.

"Hi, Bubba." Kelly pulled himself back to the present. "I'm trying to work out a timetable to show everybody was Saturday night. You know, sort of figure out if anyone could've seen something might give me a lead to Anna's killer."

"Yeah, I see what you mean. Don't know as I can help much, though. Fact is, after Anna left, I kinda petered out myself. Leroy and I had another drink, then I told him to keep the bottle and I packed it in for the night."

"So you left about ten or fifteen minutes after Anna and Cam went out?"

"Yep. It couldn't have been more'n that because they were still on the road arguing when I got outside. Fact is, I avoided them 'cause I didn't want to get involved in their argument. I cut down the path and came out up by the bridge."

"So you actually crossed the bridge before Anna and Cam ever got there?"

"Yep. Like I said, Anna was really riled about something. I figgered if she seen me, she'd give me another ration of shit."

"When you crossed the bridge, did you see any sign of Frank Perkins?"

"Nope. Wasn't anybody around. Everything was shut down. It was dark and raining like hell."

"So you went straight to your cabin and didn't see or hear anyone?"

"Hey, I said I did, didn't I? Isn't my word good enough for you?"

Kelly shook his head. "I didn't mean it like that, Bubba. I was just making sure you didn't accidentally leave anything out."

"I ain't left nothin' out." Bubba was getting agitated.

Kelly stared at the bait man. Bubba kept fidgeting with his hat and avoiding eye contact. Finally, Bubba looked at Kelly.

"You know how I felt about Anna," he muttered. "I ain't likely to forget something might help find her killer."

"I know you're not." Kelly grinned to lighten the atmosphere. "I just wanted to get the times straight and I knew you'd help as much as you could."

Bubba scuffed the ground with his boot. "Well, I better get back to the shop then." He kept his head down, still avoiding Kelly's eyes. "This weather's bringing them out in droves. I ain't had ten minutes to myself."

Kelly frowned as he watched Bubba walking back to the bait house. He was hiding something. It probably didn't have anything to do with Anna's death but whatever it was, it was sure as hell giving him a case of the guilts. Bubba looked back, spotted Kelly watching him and quickly turned away. Kelly shook his head. Bubba sure was acting strange. Maybe Leroy knew what he'd gotten in his craw.

Kelly found Leroy sitting in the Hideaway talking to Darlene, just like he did every other day of the week. Questioning him turned out to be useless. Leroy hadn't a clue what went on Saturday night.

"Ain't no use asking him." Darlene leaned over the bar to join the conversation. "He was three sheets to the wind long before midnight."

Leroy grinned sheepishly and nodded his head.

"Ask Cam," Darlene continued. "He practically had to carry Leroy out to the storage shed."

Kelly smiled. Cam had a rule that if anybody got too drunk, they went to the cot out in the storage shed and slept if off. Leroy spent more time on the cot there than he did in his own bed.

Darlene gave Kelly the names of a few stragglers who'd been in the bar at closing but there weren't many. Most of the crowd had moved on or gone home long before two o'clock.

Cam came in while they were talking.

"How's it going?" He nodded at Kelly.

"Okay. I'm finding out a few things but it's tough."

"God, what a mess." Cam filled a couple of mugs with coffee and handed one across the bar to Kelly.

"Thanks." Kelly took the mug.

Cam came around the bar and straddled a stool. "I called Bill Shipton like you said and he set up a meeting with Detective Graham." Cam took a swig of coffee and sighed clear down to his boots. "Bill agrees with you it'll be best if I tell them about last night before they dig it up. He figures they'll hold me."

Kelly nodded. "He's probably right. But hey, you expected that. I'm meeting Gus tonight and I'll try to find out where he stands."

"Thanks, Kelly. At least knowing you're digging into it gives me something to hope for."

Kelly finished his coffee, wished Cam luck with the cops, and headed back to his cabin.

Kelly stepped onto the porch where Jake was basking in the sun. "It looks like you've got more smarts than I have. For all I've found out today, I might as well have stuck with you and caught myself some rays."

Kelly dug a sack of frozen tamales out of the freezer for dinner and sliced a couple of tomatoes. He perched the plate on his lap and ate while watching the evening news. There'd been a fire at the Stockyards Hotel and some idiot in Dallas was holding a couple of clerks hostage in a 7-Eleven. Coverage of Anna's murder consisted of a wide-angle shot of the flea market accompanied by a brief interview with the sheriff, who'd summarized the facts, speculated that the motive might have been robbery and assured the public the police were questioning a number of suspects.

Kelly sighed. They were questioning suspects all right and once Cam gave his statement, he'd be at the top of their list.

The phone rang and Kelly reached for it. "Hello."

"Is this Kelly McWinter?"

"Yes, it is. What can I do for you?"

"I heard you was askin' if anybody'd seen a stranger hangin' around on Saturday night."

Kelly jerked forward in his chair. The man's voice was muffled, as if the mouthpiece was covered with a handkerchief.

"I'm listening."

"I saw some guy scopin' out the flea market along about midnight. You interested?"

"Damn straight I'm interested. Have you called the cops?"

"Ain't having nuthin' to do with no cops. If that's what you figger, I guess I'll be gettin' off the phone." The voice was agitated.

"Take it easy." Kelly attempted to calm him down. "I was just asking the obvious question. What can you tell me about this guy? Did you recognize him?"

"Nope. Can't tell y'all nuthin' about him. I got his license number though." The guy sounded like he was getting a real kick out of his chance to play James Bond.

"Good job." Kelly pulled a pen out of his pocket and reached for the notebook he kept beside the telephone. "What's the number?"

"You gonna check it out yourself?"

"Of course," Kelly lied.

"Okay. It's LQY-464."

"Got it. How can I get hold of you?"

"You can't." There was a click and the phone went dead.

Kelly tapped the cradle, got a tone and dialed Gus' home number. The caller might be a crank but if he was on the level, it could be a break for Cam.

Chapter Seven

Kelly went back to work Tuesday morning. The police were finished with the barn and all the chores he normally took care of on Sunday night after the market closed still waited. Gus would call if the license number turned up anything. At noon, Kelly broke for lunch and checked the answering machine but there'd been no calls. Either the lead was a dud, or Gus was waiting until they met for dinner to give him the news.

Kelly quit for the day at quarter past five. He was meeting Gus at six and within twenty minutes had showered, changed, and fed Jake. He headed down the hill to the garage where he kept Old Blue—the Chevy pickup he and Lynda had bought new in 1976.

An image of Lynda flashed into Kelly's mind as he got in. It didn't happen as often now, time had dulled his loss, but in those early months right after the fire, every time he'd climbed in the cab she'd been there. Long and lean and smiling like an angel, her thick blonde hair tied back in one of those gaudy scarves she loved to wear.

Kelly backed out of the garage, swung around the cabin and pulled onto Boat Club Road. He was looking forward to dinner with Gus but the return to Angelo's was stirring up powerful memories. Gus, Betty, Kelly and Lynda had gotten together there at least once a month for what Gus called their "pig outs".

Kelly supposed seeing Gus again was bringing back all these images of the past. That and his encounter with the mystery woman. She'd reminded him of Lynda, although her hair was lighter and she was a whole lot shorter. Lynda had been tall and definitely what they called leggy. Thinking of Lynda's legs brought back another memory and he laughed softly to himself.

They'd been on their way to spend a weekend in El Paso. It was mid-July and sweltering. In the middle of the afternoon, they'd stopped at a deserted rest area and taken turns splashing each other from the water fountain. After they'd cooled off, Lynda had climbed back into the truck while Kelly went to the porta-can. When he got back to the truck, he found her spread out on the seat, naked as the day she was born. It hadn't taken a rocket scientist to figure out what she had in mind. The memory spread a bittersweet pain through Kelly's body and he shifted uncomfortably in the seat.

Angelo's parking lot was crammed, just like always. Kelly spotted an empty space in the second row but he continued around back and found a spot next to the dumpster. Old Blue had earned a set of collector's plates this year and Kelly wasn't taking any chances on getting one of his doors nicked.

Kelly pushed open the door a few minutes past six. The sweet, spicy tang of Angelo's sauce wafted off the racks of ribs. His mouth watered. He picked his way carefully across the slippery sawdust covering the floor of the darkened room and headed toward a table tucked into a corner off the kitchen. Gus waved him over, a beer in one hand and a cold mug in the other.

"I waited for you like one hog waits for the other."

Kelly pulled out a chair. "Damn, those ribs smell good." The waitress approached the table and Kelly pointed to Gus' plate. "I'll have the same but throw in a couple of jalapenos."

"I see you still like that hot stuff." Gus set the rib down on his plate. "The doc said I was working myself up to an ulcer, so I've had to cut out the gut-burners."

"Yeah, well, I guess that goes along with that gray stuff you've got sprouting." Kelly grinned and ran his hands through his own thick still-brown hair.

"Your turn'll come, boy! Just you wait." Gus lifted a forkful of beans to his mouth.

"This last week's aged me at least twenty years." Kelly groaned. He thanked the waitress for his iced mug, sat it on the table, and turned back to Gus. "Now give. What about that license number?"

Gus shook his head. "Nothing much. The car's registered to a guy named Donovan Nolan. Ever heard of him?"

Kelly shook his head.

"Nolan's a sound technician and travels a lot doing the concert circuit. He's been out of town for a month and his wife says the car's been parked at the airport ever since he left. We checked. The car's out there all right with its plates still on it and the attendant says it hasn't been moved. I guess it's possible somebody took it out and brought it back without him being the wiser but it don't seem likely. We're still looking into it but I'm inclined to write your caller off as a crank."

Kelly sighed. He'd been afraid of that. "What about that news you were being so secretive about on the telephone?"

Gus grinned. "No secret. I just wanted to make sure you'd turn up. We did track down your mystery woman."

"That was quick. Who is she?"

"Her name's Krystal Davis and she's the dead woman's daughter."

"Her daughter?" Kelly frowned. "I never once heard Anna mention anything about having a kid. Are you sure about that?"

"Positive. Got a call from one of them hotshot lawyers down in Houston. He represents Davis Oil and this Krystal Davis is one of them. He hemmed and hawed about keeping her name out of the papers and all that crap but he finally gave me her phone number."

"So…what did she say?"

"I haven't talked to her yet. I called the number and got her roommate. She said Krystal would be home about eight. I figured we'd drop by after we finished up here."

"You mean you're gonna let me come along?"

"Well, since you got a good look at her, you might as well confirm it's the same woman. You can identify her, can't you?"

"Oh sure, no problem there. I was just surprised, that's all. I've been racking my brains for an excuse to talk with this gal after you'd tracked her down and here you offer it up on a platter."

"Well, if you're disappointed, I can always retract." Gus gave Kelly another broad grin.

"Like hell you will."

The waitress leaned across the table with a steaming platter of ribs. Kelly's eyes gleamed in anticipation. It felt so good sitting here eating ribs with Gus again. The atmosphere soaked into his bones and flooded him with memories.

"We had some good times in here." Gus read Kelly's mood. "Betty sends you her love. She misses you, Kelly."

"I miss her too. I miss all you guys. I'm beginning to work my way back. It took me a long time, Gus but you know how it was with Lynda and me."

"Yeah, I know. It burned my ass good at the trial. If I'd been that judge, them sons a bitches would've fried. I guess the only consolation is, they'll be so damn old when they get outta the joint, what life they have left won't be worth living."

"You know, for a long time I considered doing them myself." Kelly met Gus' eyes. "I don't know why I didn't. It sure wasn't because I cared what would happen to me. I suppose it was just all the years of being a cop. But I'm long past that now. Nothing I did to them would bring Lynda back, so I don't think about them anymore. I found out it was healthier that way."

Gus nodded.

"So, what do you think about Anna's daughter? Do you suppose she's connected with the murder?"

"I can't say until I talk to her. I wouldn't count on it, though. I'd say she's probably got a pretty tight alibi, or there's no way that lawyer would let us near her without him tagging along to hold her hand."

"No, probably not." Kelly frowned.

"You might as well go ahead and ask me what I think about that bartender friend of yours." Gus jabbed his fork in the air. "He showed up at my office this afternoon with Bill Shipton in tow. Cam said it was you who told him to get his ass in and give me a statement. I'd thank you for that if I didn't suspect you'd also had a hand in siccin' old Bill on me."

Kelly kept a straight face. "What do you think of Cam's statement?"

"I think it stinks is what I think. Had half a mind to book him right then but I decided to leave him loose until after I'd seen the woman. I know this guy's a friend of yours but what did you expect?" Gus thumped the table and glared at Kelly.

Kelly grinned. "Hey, I was just asking. I admit his story's a little loose but do you have anything specific, or is it all just speculation?"

"I've got witnesses who heard him arguing with the deceased Saturday afternoon. Then I've got his own admission he threw her out of the bar that same night, not to mention the fact he followed her outside not five minutes later."

"Sure but you've got all that from his own admission. Seems to me if Cam had anything to hide, he'd have cooked up some kind of a story about where he went after he left the bar."

Gus shook his head. "A guy named Perkins spotted Cam and Anna up on the bridge and he swears they were arguing. Your buddy probably figured he'd best come clean before this Perkins ratted on him."

"Yeah, I know all that but you still haven't placed Cam at the flea market." Kelly struggled to keep telltale signs of anger out of his voice. "I remember you always used to warn me about jumping to the obvious conclusion."

"And I'm not jumping now," Gus snapped. "He's still loose, isn't he? But don't hold your breath. This is an election year and I'm getting a lot of pressure. The public doesn't like the idea of a woman getting knocked off out at a country flea market."

111

"I'm sorry. Didn't mean to come on so strong." Kelly brushed his hand through his hair and smiled to lighten the atmosphere. "I'd appreciate it if you'd keep an open mind, though. I know Cam and I don't think he's capable of murder. He can be a hot head at times but inside he's a marshmallow. Like his financial problems. He wouldn't have any if he'd quit carrying all those old-timers on a tab. He's a pushover for hard luck stories and whenever one of the Creek folks gets into a bind, Cam's the first one to stick his hand in his pocket."

Gus started to speak and Kelly hurried on so he wouldn't be interrupted. "Look, I'm not trying to bleed all over the table. Anna was a friend of mine. If Cam killed her, he deserves to get nailed. I just don't want to see him railroaded by a lot of circumstantial evidence."

"Nice speech." Gus chewed on a rib and swallowed. "What I'm wondering is, where the hell is all this leading?"

Kelly grinned. Gus knew him too well. "I'd like to work with you on this one. I know you're under a lot of pressure and I think I can help. I'd be sort of an unofficial snoop. That way I could help you get your nose into what's going on down there."

Gus shook his head but Kelly kept talking. "I won't interfere with your investigation. You know me better than that. But I do have some advantages you don't. I know those Creek people. I've been living with them for five years now and they treat me like one of their own.

"You know how it is, Gus. Country folks always have a few things to hide. Somebody's got a still out in the bushes or a fella's doing a bit of night fishing, stuff like that. They're conditioned not to talk to the police. Even if they do know anything, nine times out of ten they'll keep their mouths shut rather than tell it to a cop."

Gus had stopped shaking his head but he was still frowning. "You've got a point about those Creek folks. It's like pulling hen's teeth to get information out of them. If I go along with you on this, we'll need a clear understanding."

Gus paused and waited until Kelly nodded. "You aren't a cop anymore." Gus kept his eyes on Kelly's face. "My ass'll be on the line here. One screw-up on your part and I can kiss my job goodbye."

"I know that and it's not going to happen." Kelly met the detective's steady gaze. "Sure, Cam's a friend of mine and I want to help him if I can. But he's not the same kind of friend you are. He hasn't been around me my whole life. You ought to know I'd cut off both my arms before I'd stir up anything that'd land you in a pile of shit."

"It's against my better judgment." Gus shook his head again. "But I'll go along with you for now. I'll tell you as much as I think you need to know and I want your word you'll check with me before you so much as piss in the Creek. If you can live with that, then we've got a deal."

"Thanks." Kelly nodded, then stood up and grinned. "I gotta take a leak. You wanna come along?"

"Asshole!" Gus drained his beer. "Get your business done and let's get over to Camp Bowie and see what that gal's got to say.

Chapter Eight

Penny raced across the room and grabbed Krystal's arms the minute she cleared the apartment door. "Policeman call." Her cold fingers tightened. "He want to know when you come home. I say eight o'clock. He come soon."

"That's okay." Krystal smiled at her panicky roommate. "Uncle Andrew called our lawyer. Mr. Masters already called the police and explained why I was at the flea market."

"They no come?"

"Oh, they'll still come but it's nothing to worry about. They'll just ask us where we were and what we did Saturday night."

"They question me too?"

Krystal flinched from the bite of Penny's fingers. "All they'll do is ask you to confirm I was here all night. I'm sure they'll be very nice to you."

Penny's head shook back and forth. "Have police come very bad thing. Lose much face."

"Don't worry about that, not here. In America, it's not a disgrace for the police to talk to you. The neighbors might be a bit curious but we certainly won't lose face over it."

"I no talk to policeman."

"You have to. Just tell them I went to bed early and you stayed home and watched television."

Penny shook her head again. "I don't stay home, Krissie. Adelle, from upstairs, asked do I want to watch movies. I go there."

"You did?" Krystal's eyes widened. "I thought you were here all night. When did you leave?"

"You long time sleeping. Maybe eleven."

"What time did you get home?"

"Movie end very late, two o'clock. Lying to policeman not good. I go shopping."

"No. You can't do that. They'll just come back, or they might pick you up and take you to the police station." Krystal pried Penny's fingers loose and sat down at the table. "This is awful," she said. "I told Uncle Andrew I had an alibi. It's not your fault but I wish you hadn't gone anywhere."

Penny slid into the other chair and sat watching Krystal then she spoke. "Policeman not know Adelle. I say nothing. Not lie. Only not to say."

"Oh, Penny." Relief flooded Krystal's face. "I don't want to get you into any trouble but I hate to think what they'll do if they find out I was home alone."

Penny bobbed her head. "I speak little English. They no understand. Now, we forget about policeman. Tell me about uncle. Was he very angry?"

"Oh, he was okay. In fact, he was quite nice about it. He didn't like it that I'd gone to a detective but he was so relieved I had an alibi that he forgot to lecture me."

"He tell why mother run away?"

"No, but he said we'd talk about it later. I think he was sorry. I don't know, Penny. I'm so confused. All I have of my mother is childish memories and they're all mixed up. I've always believed they made her leave but now I don't know what to believe. Seeing her was such an awful experience. I don't even know how I feel anymore."

"She give you much pain. Talk with uncle good thing. Make you feel better."

The doorbell rang. Krystal paused halfway across the floor and looked at Penny. "That must be the police. Will you be okay?"

Penny nodded. "I go wait." She headed for the living room.

Krystal opened the door as much as the length the chain allowed and peered through the crack at the two men outside.

"Miss Krystal Davis?" Gus held out his identification card.

117

"Yes." Krystal released the chain and swung open the door. "Come in, please."

"Thank you, ma'am." Gus stepped past her. "I'm Detective Graham and this is Kelly McWinter. Perhaps you recognize him?"

"Yes." She closed the door. "From the flea market."

"That's right. I brought him along in case there's anything we need to clarify about what happened on Saturday."

"I see." She turned and led the way along the hall into the living room. "This is Penny, my roommate."

"Ma'am," Gus acknowledged the introduction.

Penny nodded and quickly averted her eyes.

"Will you have a seat?" Krystal offered.

Kelly selected a straight back chair.

"There's no need to be nervous about this, Miss Davis." Gus sank into a large armchair. "We'll just have a little chat about what happened out at the flea market."

Kelly'd always admired the way Gus handled an investigation. He had that "Y'all-just-set-yourself-down-a-spell-and-chat" kind of atmosphere down pat. It worked every time. If someone had guilty knowledge, Gus' approach put them at ease and made them careless. If they were innocent, it kept them happy and made for good police relations.

"Do you want to know why I was out there?" Krystal asked.

"I've heard what the lawyer said but I'd rather hear it from you. Just take your time and tell us what you remember."

"I suppose you've already found out she was my mother?"

"I understand you were estranged." Gus smiled to soften the remark.

Krystal glanced over at Penny then turned to speak to Kelly. "You must think I'm a fool after what I did out there."

Kelly shook his head. "You looked like you were having a rough time of it."

"We both understand your feelings," Gus said, pulling her attention back to his question. "Don't worry about what we think. Just tell us in your own words what happened after you decided to try and find your mother."

"It's a long story and hard to explain but I'll try."

Speaking softly, dragging the memories out of her past, Krystal told them about her father's suicide and her mother's disappearance, her attempts to trace her mother, her uncle's refusal to discuss the past and her decision to hire a detective. Finally, she talked about her trip to the flea market and her abortive attempt to speak with her mother.

"It was horrible." Her hands clenched into fists. "This nasty, little man came in the shop while I was watching. He bumped into me and nearly knocked me off my feet. Then he went up to my mother and gave her this brown paper bag. And then my mother opened the bag and pulled out a bottle of whiskey. I was horrified. And every time I think about my mother guzzling out of that whiskey bottle, it makes me sick to my stomach."

She shivered and Kelly felt it in his stomach. *God, she reminds me of Lynda.* He gave himself a mental shake and focused his attention on Gus.

"I understand," Gus said. "You don't have to go into any more detail. I take it seeing your mother drinking out of the bottle was what prompted you to rush at her the way you did?"

Krystal nodded. "I wanted to get the bottle away from her. Like that would've changed anything."

Gus scribbled rapidly in his notebook. "Okay, I don't think we need to go into that any further. What about after you left the flea market? Did you come straight back to the apartment?"

Krystal nodded. "I didn't want anyone to see me. I drove home as soon as I'd pulled myself together enough. I talked to Penny for a few minutes. And then I took a couple of sleeping pills and went to bed."

"You were home when she got here?" Gus turned to Penny.

She nodded, keeping her eyes on the floor. "Krissie come home, cry long time. She take pills. Sleep all night."

"I see." Gus turned back to Krystal. "I wonder if you can help me fix the times. Kelly here thought it was about five when you had your encounter with Anna. Does that seem right?"

"I guess so. I didn't really notice. It was after four when I got to the flea market but it took me awhile to get the courage to approach my mother. Why? Is it important?"

Gus ignored the question. "Do you remember what time you got home?"

"I don't know." She shook her head. "I couldn't drive at first. I sat in the car and cried."

Gus looked at Penny.

Keeping her eyes on the floor she said. "I look at clock very much. Seven o'clock, Krissie come home."

Gus sat forward in the chair and spoke to both of them. "Then you spent the evening at home, is that right?"

"I think it was about eight-thirty when I went to bed." Krystal's voice was strained but she answered without hesitation. "I got up once to go to the bathroom. Penny was watching television."

"Is that right?" Gus turned to Penny. "You spent the entire evening watching television?"

Penny bobbed her head up and down. "I am quiet. Watch television very late. Maybe three in morning."

"Then you confirm Miss Davis' statement that she was home all night."

"Krissie sleep long time. No get up."

"Well, you've both been very helpful. Now, there's just one more thing. I wonder if you could identify this." He pulled an envelope out of his jacket pocket and removed the bright red scarf.

"That's my scarf!" Krystal stretched out her hand. "I lost it at the flea market. How did you get it?"

Gus pulled his hand back. "It's difficult to tell you this but it can't be helped. I'm afraid I'll have to keep the scarf for a while because the murderer used it to strangle Mrs. Davis."

Krystal gasped and dropped her head. Blond hair spilled forward and covered her face. She didn't make a sound but her shoulders started shaking.

Penny jumped up and ran to her side. "No, Krissie. Not your fault. You lose scarf."

Krystal lifted her head and stared at Gus. Her eyes were watery and her voice trembled. "That filthy little man who was talking to my mother—the one who gave her the whiskey. Maybe he took it."

"What man? Can you describe him?"

"I didn't really look at him. He smelled like fish. He was short and his legs were bowed. I don't remember his face. I just didn't notice. I was looking at my mother."

Gus shifted himself out of the armchair. "You've been very helpful. I'm sorry we had to stir up unhappy memories but I appreciate your frankness. I'll leave my card and if you think of anything else, I'd appreciate a call."

Kelly stood. "I'm sorry." Krystal raised her eyes. "Maybe I can give you a ring later. I knew Anna pretty well. If you'd like to talk about her, I'd be happy to share what I know."

"Thank you," she said. "I'd like that."

"You know the guy she was talking about?" Gus asked as they walked back to the car.

"Bubba. But if you think he had anything to do with strangling Anna, you can forget it. Bubba couldn't lie worth a damn if his life depended on it. Shows all over his face. I've talked to him about it a couple of times, not just once. If he was hiding something about Anna's murder, I'da damn sure known."

"Greed does strange things to people," Gus said. "We're already checking him out anyway. One of your Creek people told us Bubba had a falling out with Anna over some fish camp he wanted to buy."

"Frank Perkins, of course." Kelly sighed. "If there's any shit to start you can always count on Frank. Sure, Bubba and Anna'd been talking about buying a fish camp for a long time. They had words that night but it was booze talk. Anna was temperamental when she got to drinking and Bubba knew it."

"I'll keep that in mind." Gus pulled his car up beside Old Blue and turned to face Kelly. "I'm running a check on everybody out there, especially the ones hanging around the Hideaway that night. If I come up with anything, I'll give you a call. In the meantime, keep your ears open and let me know what you hear."

"Will do," Kelly said. "And thanks for the ribs. Next time, they'll be on me."

Kelly didn't hit Indian Creek till after ten but he knew Cam would be waiting for news, so he stopped at the Hideaway. Leroy and Marty played cribbage at their usual table. Otherwise, the bar was empty. Kelly sat on a bar stool and Cam reached in the cooler for a Budweiser.

"Anything new?"

"Gus found the mystery woman." Kelly propped his arms on the counter. "She wasn't much help though."

"I see." Cam's face dropped.

"It's not hopeless. She gave us a couple of leads I'm going to follow up. That's more than I had before I went there. Krystal—that's her name—is Anna's daughter and from what she had to say, I' got an idea Anna's past could stand some looking into."

"I'll be damned." Cam's eyes widened and he shook his head in disbelief. "I never figgered Anna for having a kid. How come she never came around before?"

"Seems Anna took off when Krystal was seven and left her with her grandmother. Krystal hired a detective a couple weeks ago and he tracked Anna down."

Cam frowned. "There was a fella named Boscon nosing around out here. He claimed to be writing a story for some fishing magazine. I wondered about him at the time. He asked a lot of questions and most of them had nothing to do with fishing."

"That's the guy. He told Krystal about Anna's stall at the flea market and she came out to look. She was waiting for a chance to talk to Anna when Bubba showed up with a bottle of whiskey."

Cam grinned. "Sounds like Bubba."

"Yep! You know how Anna was. She tipped the bottle right there in her stall and started guzzling. Seems Krystal snapped when she saw that. She tried to grab the bottle and fell into Anna's chair."

"Do you believe her?"

"Yeah. Her story pretty much jives with what I saw. It's her family situation that's got me curious. Krystal always wondered what happened to her mother, I mean, who wouldn't? But nobody in the family would talk about it. All she knows is that her father committed suicide and her mother disappeared the same night."

"Sounds like a can of worms."

"Got a nasty smell all right. So I'm planning to dig around in the past a bit and I think I'll start with her husband's suicide."

"Maybe Anna killed him."

Kelly shook his head. "I doubt it. The police are damn good and thorough when one of the rich crowd commits suicide. What I can't figure is why Anna walked out on his estate the way she did."

"That doesn't sound like Anna."

"That's what I mean. She was tight about money. I'd have expected her to fight like a tiger to hold onto what was hers."

"I always had a feeling there was something strange about Anna moving here."

"What do you mean strange?"

"You weren't around when she first came to the Creek. She was a real looker then. Lots of class. Most of us thought she was running away from a bad marriage. Funny! I knew her damn near eighteen years and she never talked about her past."

"Anna knew how to keep her mouth shut." Kelly set his beer can back on the counter. "I'm going to call it a night now but don't give up hope. I offered to meet with Krystal and tell her what I know about Anna. She seemed to like the idea, so I'm hoping we can get together."

Chapter Nine

First thing Wednesday morning, Kelly called Krystal's number.

"Krystal, Kelly McWinter. If you're sure you'd like to talk about your mother—I was thinking dinner? Tonight?"

"I'd love to."

"Where'd you like to go?"

"Surprise me. Seven?"

"See you then."

Kelly turned to Jake after he hung up and grinned. "Looks like I've got me a date. I wonder where I ought to take her. Maybe Martini's out on the lake. They've got a great view and the tables are set up nice. The food's good too."

Jake shoved his head against Kelly's leg to keep him scratching and Kelly laughed. "You'd pay more attention if it was a female shepherd I was talking about, wouldn't you, boy? I'll give Martini's a call, then we'll go for a walk. And remind me I still gotta talk to Frank, okay?"

There was a crisp chill in the air and they set a fast pace toward the Hideaway. The grass along the roadside had faded to brown and the trees were in full fall finery. A couple of pickups honked as they passed and Kelly waved. At the top of the hill, a car pulled up beside them and stopped.

"Getting your exercise?" Gus leaned his head out the window.

"Good for the paunch." Kelly grinned and patted his flat stomach. "What are you doing out this way?"

"One of the boys searching Anna's cabin turned up a metal box. Looks like it's been rifled pretty good, too. I'm going over to take a look. You want to come along?"

"You bet. Okay if Jake rides?"

"Sure. Let him in." Gus motioned to the back seat.

Kelly settled Jake and folded himself into the passenger side. "Any sign of a break-in?"

"Nope. Whoever did it was real good or had a key. Know any possibilities?" Gus took his eyes off the road and gave Kelly a sharp glance.

"Well, Bubba, of course, but I can't see him searching her cabin. Maybe she left the door unlocked. That's not uncommon out here."

"Could be but it still gives me one more reason to have a little talk with your friend Bubba."

"Why don't you let me talk to him? Bubba's always been straight with me. If he knows anything, I'll let you know and you can pull him in for an official grilling."

"I dunno. I'll think about it. Let's take a look inside first. Maybe you'll notice something out of kilter. You been inside before, haven't you?" Gus pulled up in front of a small pine slab cabin. The front door stood open, a deputy framing the doorway.

"Sure, but I never paid much attention to what she had in the place."

"Howdy, Fred," Gus greeted the deputy. "Where's the box?"

"Over here, sir." The deputy led them into a small, wood-paneled bedroom. The bed was shoved aside and a floorboard was pried up, leaving a hole in the floor. A green metal ammunition box sat on the floor next to the hole. "You can see the lock's been pried off." Fred pointed to a small padlock hanging, still locked, on the lock plate of the box. "Looks like somebody used a pry bar on it."

"What's this stuff?" Gus indicated a pile of papers stacked alongside the box.

"The thick one's her will. The rest of it's all financial stuff—stock reports, bonds, the works. There's a couple of bank statements. Wait'll you get a load of the balances on them suckers."

"Have the lab boys finished going over the place?"

"Yep. They wrapped it up just before I called you."

"Okay. I'll take things from here. You and Mike head back in. I'll bring the papers along when I'm done."

Gus picked up a thick envelope stamped as 'Last Will and Testament' in dark fancy calligraphy. He pulled out the Will and scanned the pages.

"Take a look at this." He handed the will to Kelly. "Except for a couple of bequests, she's left the whole lot to Krystal. Of course, since we know she's the daughter, that's natural enough but read the third paragraph."

Kelly scanned the page to find the passage Gus had indicated. "In the event that my said daughter, Krystal Marie Davis, is not living at the time of my death, or is prevented for any reason whatsoever from claiming the proceeds of my estate, I designate my good friend and companion, James Bubba Tate, to be the recipient of the residue of my estate."

"Nothing strange about that." Kelly handed the document back to Gus. "Bubba and Anna been together a long time."

"Looks like she left a nice chunk of change." Gus swept his arm across the stack of papers spread out on the floor.

"Yeah, well, there's always been talk about Anna having money hidden away out here. I knew she was smarter than that." Kelly picked up one of the passbooks. "Seems she was a pretty shrewd investor."

"I wonder if Bubba knew about this."

"What difference does it make?" Kelly shrugged. "Krystal's very much alive and she gets the bundle. Now if Krystal had been the one murdered, you might be justified in wondering about Bubba."

"Providing nothing happens to Krystal between now and when they probate the estate."

"Horse shit."

Gus let out a chuckle, then folded the will and put it back in the envelope. "Don't get your tail in a knot. I'm just looking at all the angles. I'll tell you something I am wondering about. I don't see any sign of that note your friend Cam was so het up about. That strikes me as odd. It's the kind of thing you'd expect to find with the rest of this stuff. You got any ideas?"

"I don't know." Kelly frowned. "Maybe Bill Shipton's got it. Do you want me to ask Cam?"

"No. You stay away from him. I'll take care of that end. Go have a talk with Bubba. Find out what he knows about this will and that scarf. I'm going to dig around here awhile. I'll get back to you later tonight or in the morning."

"Okay. If it's tonight, you'll have to leave a message on the machine. I've got a dinner date with Krystal."

"Didn't waste any time, huh?"

Kelly blushed. "She's a nice kid. Besides, I want to find out a little more about the Davis clan and what happened between them and Anna."

"Just watch your step. The Davises are in a position to cause me a few headaches and I don't need that right now."

"Don't worry. I won't cause any flack. I'll slip a few pointed questions into the conversation and watch her reaction. If she gets skittish, I'll back off."

"Yeah, you make sure you do that. Now get the hell out of here and let me do some work."

Kelly stepped out the door and whistled. Jake bounded out of the woods and they headed down to the creek.

The bait house was deserted but the door was open, so Bubba wouldn't have gone far. Kelly leaned back in a chair and propped his feet against a fish tank. It was relaxing inside. Once you got used to the smell.

Before they'd found the metal box, Kelly hadn't been too concerned about what Bubba was holding back. Now he needed to know what it was but Bubba was inclined to be touchy when you questioned his word. Kelly pondered his approach while he waited.

Bubba walked in and stepped over to the fish tank with a large pail in his hand.

"Hey, Kelly, whatcha' you doing here?"

"I just dropped by for a chat. What have you got there?" Kelly pointed at the pail.

"Minnows. I can't keep enough of these suckers in the tanks this time of year. Hang on a sec while I dump them in the trough, then I'll grab a coffee with you."

Kelly grabbed a couple mugs from the shelf, lifted the pot off the stove and poured them each a cup of Bubba's brew.

"When you gonna break down and buy a drip pot, Bubba? Like that's ever gonna happen."

"Dang sure ain't. I ain't having nothing to do with that watered-down, lukewarm shit comes outta them fancy pots. So whatcha' you been up to?" Bubba pulled up a stool and took the mug Kelly handed over.

"Just nosing around. I found out something that might interest you. Anna had a daughter she hadn't seen in eighteen years."

"So you found out about the kid."

"You mean you knew?"

Bubba shrugged. "Anna had some lines you didn't cross and the kid was one of 'em. I respected that. She never came out and talked about her daughter but yeah, I knew she had one. You don't think the kid killed her, do you?"

"No, nothing like that. Her name's Krystal and all she wanted to do was find out why her mother deserted her. She's sure started me wondering about why Anna took off the way she did and I plan to try and find some answers."

"I hope you find something. I know damn well Cam didn't kill Anna. The cops probably think he did but they don't know Cam. He can't even watch me gut fish. No way could he strangle anyone—'specially not an old friend like Anna."

"Well, they've got to go by the evidence. That and what they find out from talking to friends and relatives. By the way, the police went through Anna's cabin and found a metal box stashed under the floorboard in her bedroom. You wouldn't know anything about that box, would you?"

"What makes you think I'd know anything about it?" Bubba narrowed his eyes.

"Because you knew Anna better than anybody else and I figured she might've told you."

"Yeah, I knew about it. So what?"

"So somebody busted the lock and went through Anna's papers, that's what."

"And you think it was me that busted into her box?" Bubba glared.

Kelly snapped right back. "Don't be so damn touchy. I figured you'd rather talk to me than get hauled down to the station and talk to Gus. If I was wrong, tell me now. I didn't say you broke into the box but I did figure you might have an idea who did."

"How should I know?" Bubba hunched up his shoulders and rested his chin on his collarbone.

The bait man was dodging and Kelly was sick of it. "What is this crap, Bubba? I had to do plenty of talking to get Gus to let me question you about this. I figured you'd be grateful. So what happens? I come in here to ask a few civil questions and you give me a ration of shit. I don't know what's got into you lately but I'm beginning to wonder what the hell you do know about Anna's murder."

"Hey, I'm sorry." Bubba's face turned red. "I didn't mean to give you a rough time. I know you're trying to help Cam outta a hole but I don't want to end up taking his place."

"I sure understand that, Bubba, but you're only making it worse by copping an attitude."

"Okay, I get the message." Bubba's lips twitched into a sheepish grin. "Yeah, I knew about Anna's box and no, I didn't break into it.

Wouldn't have had to." Bubba reached into his pocket and pulled out a key ring. "Got a key."

He selected a small silver key took it off the ring and handed it over. "You can check it yourself. When Anna made that note with Cam, she stashed it away in her box. Then she showed me where she kept it, gave me a key and said if anything was to happen to her, I should get the note and tear it up."

"Did Cam know where she kept the note?"

"I don't think so but I can't be sure. There's something I need to tell you and you ain't gonna like it much." Bubba paused and took a sip of coffee. "I wanted to tell you earlier but I was afraid of making things worse for Cam. See, I went to Anna's cabin to tear up the note like she said. The box was outta the hole, just like you said. And when I looked through the papers, the note, well—it was gone."

"You read Anna's will?"

"Yeah, I read it. I know my name's in it. But what the hell? The daughter's alive. Nobody's got any call to think I bumped Anna off to get hold of her money."

"Nobody's thinking that Bubba. We're just trying to piece everything together and find out what happened down there."

"Well, you know everything I do now. Sorry I didn't tell you about the box earlier but damn.

Kinda between a rock and hard place. I figured blabbing about that note would be the same as putting a noose around Cam's neck. I even thought about hiding the box but I was scared the cops would find out."

"Good thinking." Kelly shook his head. "You're right about me not liking what you say about the note. Gus was already wondering why it wasn't with Anna's papers and when he finds out you went through that box looking for it, he'll rake you over the coals good."

"Do we have to tell him?"

"Damn straight we have to tell him," Kelly snapped. "And the sooner the better. Your prints are on that box. I'm just wondering if Cam's prints are there too. I'd sure like to ask him a few questions but Gus told me to stay away from Cam."

"Gus ain't said nothing to me." Bubba grinned.

"I didn't hear that. But if you do happen to run into Cam, you might mention whoever took that note probably left their prints all over the box and they'd better come clean with Gus in a hurry."

"Gottcha! I think I'll close up here and mosey on down to the Hideaway. I'll catch you later."

"One more thing." Kelly raised his voice. "I promised Gus I'd ask if you saw a red scarf around Anna's stall after that ruckus with Krystal Saturday afternoon."

"No, didn't see no scarf." Bubba frowned and the puzzled look on his face was answer enough.

"Okay, it's not important. Just something I told Gus I'd check on. I'll catch you later." Kelly moved toward the door. "You might pass the word—anybody knows anything about Anna's murder, they'd best come clean. Cops don't have a sense of humor where murder's concerned and it pisses them off when they catch people lying."

Satisfied, Kelly said goodbye to Bubba and headed back to the cabin. It was past five and if he was going to pick up Krystal at seven, he'd have to hustle.

Thirty minutes later, showered, shaved and dressed in slim cut slacks and a dark blue sport coat, Kelly gave his hair a once-over with the blow dryer, added a splash of cologne and stepped up to the mirror. He'd had a few casual dates since Lynda died but nothing special. This was the first time and already he found himself fighting butterflies. Of course, this wasn't really a date but all the same, the tension was there.

"You'd think I was back in high school," he stopped to give Jake a pat. Jake flopped his tail and watched Kelly go out the door.

Kelly sped up the hill, then hit the brakes. Two police cars were parked in front of the Hideaway and Bubba stood on the steps with his hands in his pockets. Kelly pulled onto the shoulder. Spotting him, Bubba dashed across the road and jumped into the truck.

"Well, you was right," Bubba croaked. "The shit's hit the fan."

"What happened?"

"The cops showed up twenty minutes ago. With a search warrant. They took Cam back to his place. It weren't more'n five minutes before they brought him back out and took off in one of the cruisers. I guess they've arrested him."

"Did you get a chance to ask Cam about that box?"

"Yep and it's like I figured. He went up to Anna's cabin after they had that fight up on the bridge. Cam claims he didn't bust open the box though. Says he found it open same as I did."

Kelly frowned and shook his head. "Damn fool! Did he say what he did with the note?"

"Oh, hell yeah! He put it in his desk. The cops came while I was still talking to him, so he didn't have a chance to get it outta there."

"What's going on now?" Kelly pointed at the police cars.

"They're talking to Darlene and looking around the Hideaway. They didn't bother the rest of us none. It was Cam they wanted."

"Well, I'm late, so I've gotta get going. I'll give Gus a call in the morning."

"Okay. They haven't asked me nothing yet but I guess I gotta tell them when they do, huh?"

"You tell them the truth, Bubba. Won't help Cam a damn bit for you to get yourself tossed in a cell alongside of him."

As he pulled away from Bubba, Kelly shook his head in disgust. "Goddam Cam!"

Chapter Ten

Krystal's blonde hair was tied back with a narrow black band, a simple act of mourning in her mother's memory. It touched Kelly's heart.

"You seem a little more rested tonight," he said, as he helped her into the truck.

She smiled, a pink flush tinting her cheeks. "After you and Detective Graham left, Penny chased me to bed. I was asleep the minute my head touched the pillow."

"Well, good. A good night's sleep sure put the roses back in your cheeks." Kelly's eyes lingered admiringly and Krystal's flush deepened.

"You must've thought I was horrible when you saw me in that scene with my mother." She lowered her eyes and twisted a strand of hair.

"Not horrible. Scared. I saw the panic in your eyes when you came to. I really wanted to pick you up and give you a hug but being strangers, I wasn't sure you'd misunderstood." He gave Krystal a grin and she answered with a shy smile.

"I'm embarrassed about the way I acted."

"Hey, you had good reason for the way you acted." Kelly reached over and patted her

142

shoulder. "Now let's forget about that meeting and enjoy ourselves. Okay?"

"Yes, please." She smiled and her eyes sparkled. "Where are we going?"

"A little place on the lake called Martini's. You ever been there?"

"No, I've never even heard of it. What's it like?"

"You'll see pretty soon. It's over on the far side of Eagle Mountain Lake."

Krystal leaned back in her seat and Kelly concentrated on his driving until he pulled off Jacksboro highway onto the access road that followed the lake.

"Do you like seafood?" he broke the silence.

"Of course. I'm from Houston."

"That's what I figured. Good thing I was right. Martini's has the best seafood around these parts."

The parking lot was full so Kelly drove around the lot and backed into a spot against the fence.

"I hope you don't mind a little hike." He hopped out of the truck and circled around to open her door. "Old Blue's sensitive to nicks."

"Of course not. I don't blame you for being careful. It's a beautiful truck. What year is it?"

"It's a '76. I've spent a fair amount of time patching and polishing."

"It shows." She admired the spectacle of Martini's framed against the glistening lake. "I'd no idea they had a place like this in Fort Worth. It's more what I'd expect to find in Houston."

"It does look a bit like it belongs on the ocean," Kelly took her hand and led her toward the long, low structure spread gracefully along the lakeshore. The soft gray of the paint combined with the white trim of the base suggested whitecaps beating against a rocky cliff.

"I reserved us a table by the windows," Kelly smiled down at her. "I figured it was too chilly for an outdoor table but it's nice the way they've set it up inside. Gives you the feeling you're sitting on the water. The architect was probably from Houston." He released her hand to let her precede him through the front door.

A hostess escorted them to a small alcove set off from the main dining room. A bank of greenery secluded the table. The aquarium beside them was stocked with tropical fish.

Krystal's eyes sparkled approval. "This is really charming." She pointed to the seamless pane of glass overlooking the lake. "I feel like I could reach down and trail my fingers in the water."

"I'm glad you like it." Kelly opened the menu and scanned the entrees. "Do you want me to order for us?"

"Yes, please do. I love seafood. Anything you choose will be fine with me."

"Okay. We'll start with hot, spiced shrimp and Margaritas but we'll wait a while before I order the main course. Does that suit you?"

"Perfect. It's so peaceful here. It'll be easy to talk. I do want to hear about my mother. My grandmother never allowed me to mention her and Uncle Andrew was just as bad. Stella used to bring her up sometimes—when nobody else was around. She'd say things like 'blood will tell,' and 'you'll probably turn out just like your mother', but she was just being nasty."

"Stella's your aunt?"

"Well, she's Uncle Andrew's wife, so I guess she's my aunt but we definitely aren't close. She was a barmaid when she met Uncle Andrew and as far as I'm concerned, she still is."

"She married your uncle after you went to live with him?"

"No, before. I lived with my grandmother until I was fifteen. We moved in with Uncle Andrew when Grandmother Davis developed Alzheimer's. She didn't approve of Stella but toward the end, she didn't know who any of us were."

"I guess it was tough being raised without a mother."

"My grandmother definitely wasn't the motherly type." Krystal's tone edged toward bitterness. Kelly figured life with grandmother must have been pretty grim.

"Doesn't sound like much fun."

"Oh, I got used to it."

"I've heard in the early stages of Alzheimer's a person's often confused between the past and the present. Did your grandmother mention your mother after she took sick?"

"Well, sort of. Sometimes she thought I was my mother. She'd say things I didn't understand. She wasn't a nice old woman, you know." Her eyes flashed with strong emotion, quickly harnessed. Kelly changed the subject.

"Tell me about your Uncle Andrew. Are you close to him?"

"No. I've never been close to my family. I like Uncle Andrew better than Stella, though. He's never been mean to me and he doesn't dig at me the way she does. Of course, he does resent my company stock. When my father died, all his shares went into my trust. Then my grandmother left me hers, too, and that surprised me as much as it did Uncle Andrew. He's never said anything to me but I heard him talking to

146

Stella after Grandmother Davis' will was read and he was furious."

"That means you control the business, doesn't it?"

"I suppose so. I own most of the stock but it doesn't matter. I don't have any interest in the company, so Uncle Andrew runs everything anyhow."

"Maybe you'll change your mind when you finish school."

"I doubt it. I'm going to work with emotionally disturbed children. I couldn't care less about the business. We've gotten off the track, though. You were going to tell me about my mother. Please."

"Of course." Kelly smiled and took a sip of his drink. "I'm trying to think where to start. I wasn't exactly on intimate terms with Anna. Nobody was except Bubba. He was her special friend, you know. He knew her better than any of us."

"That dirty little man?" Krystal wrinkled her nose.

"Well, I suppose he might look that way to an outsider but he's really an okay guy. Oh, he drinks too much—so did Anna—but you had to know them to get beyond their drinking problems."

Krystal flinched and Kelly regretted his words.

"What I mean is, they had their own charm. Anna was cantankerous and ornery, especially when she was drinking but she was also remarkably kind and understanding. She didn't wear her good deeds like a badge the way some folks do but she did plenty of them. I know several families at Indian Creek who won't eat near as well now Anna's not around to stock their cupboards. Then there's Cam. The fellow who owns the Hideaway. He would've lost his business a couple of years back if Anna hadn't come to the rescue."

"Where did she get the money?"

"I don't know. I suspect your uncle can tell you more about that than I can. I'm not really supposed to say anything but you'll be finding out soon anyhow. Anna had a lot of money when she died and she left it to you."

Krystal stared at him. "I don't believe it."

"It's true. I don't know why Anna took off when you were a child but I don't believe for a minute it was because she didn't love you. She left you everything. And I'm sure she loved you a lot."

"She didn't look to me like she had any money."

"Well, she did. And the only people mentioned in her will were you and Bubba. He's the alternate heir. In the event you didn't survive Anna."

"That man?"

"You need to meet Bubba. You've only seen his bad side. Bubba could charm the stinger off a hornet if he had a mind to it."

Krystal tried to smile but it wasn't very convincing.

"Anyway, your uncle seems like the logical source for all this money Anna's been getting. And the fact that he won't tell you anything about why she left the family has me puzzled."

"You think he had something to do with her death?"

"No. I just think he knows something about Anna that might point toward her killer and I'm trying to figure a way to find out what it is."

"I don't think I want to talk about it anymore." Krystal turned her head toward the window.

"I'm sorry. What say we order and I promise, no more questions."

Kelly lifted his arm and signaled the waitress to take their orders. "We'll have the blackened redfish with crawdad *etouffé* and a bottle of Llano Estacado cabernet sauvignon," he said when she approached the table.

"Thank you." Krystal turned back to Kelly. Her eyes shone with unnatural brightness but the tears were under control.

Kelly reached for her hand and stroked her fingers. "That was thoughtless on my part," he said. "We all have our hot buttons. After we get to know each other better—and I hope we will—you'll find I've got a few of my own."

"I'd like that." She smiled. "So tell me something about yourself. We've talked enough about me."

"There's not much to tell. I'm what they call a homegrown Texan. I was born in Fort Worth—lived here all my life. I married my high school sweetheart and joined the police force. Lynda, that was my wife's name, died a few years back and I kinda lost interest in things. I quit the force and took a job as security guard out at Indian Creek. I've been there ever since."

"I'm sorry about your wife. That must've been really hard." Her fingers tightened around his hand.

Her soothing voice brought a lump to Kelly's throat. Even after all this time, he still had trouble sharing the pain. "It took me a long time to come to terms with losing her. I don't talk about it much." He mumbled the words, his voice gruff with emotion.

"I've never loved anyone, so I can't imagine that kind of pain." A wistful note of longing shaded her voice. Loneliness peeped through her eyes.

"You're a beautiful woman," he pulled his thoughts away from his own pain. "One of these days, some lucky guy will come along and teach you all about love."

"I don't know," she shook her head and locked her eyes with his. "I wonder if I'd even know how to share that kind of love." She dropped her eyes. "I don't really feel anything about my mother, you know. Oh, I'm sad because she's dead but it's a selfish sadness. I'm mainly sorry because I never got to ask her why she went off and left me. I keep thinking I ought to feel some kind of personal loss but I don't."

"Of course you don't. You were just a child when she left. It hurt you to the quick. As the years went by, you built up walls to protect yourself. You can't be expected to grieve for her when you never had a chance to know her. Or for her to explain why she left."

"Why do you think she was killed?"

Kelly took a sip of wine. "I don't know why she was killed, Krystal. I think the police believe my friend Cam killed her because they had a falling out over the note she had on his bar. They had a fight about it the night Anna died, so it looks bad for him. But I don't believe he did it. Actually, I'd like to ask for your help in finding out some things that might lead to her killer. If you feel up to talking about it."

"Yes. I want to know the truth. But how can I help? I don't know anything about my mother except what I read in Mr. Boscon's report and what you and Detective Graham have told me."

"I know you don't but you know about your uncle and your family in Houston and I can't help feeling Anna's past has something to do with her murder."

"But nobody except Penny even knew I'd found my mother until after she was dead."

"What about the detective you hired to find her?"

"Mr. Boscon? But what would he have to do with my mother's death?"

"Probably nothing but the Davis family is pretty well-known around these parts. It's not impossible Mr. Boscon might've called your uncle and told him he'd found your mother."

"Uncle Andrew." The pain was back in Krystal's voice. "So you do think he killed my mother."

"No." Kelly reached out and took her hand again. "I just think there's a possibility he knew you'd found her. Maybe he told somebody about

152

it and that somebody had a reason for keeping you and your mother apart."

She frowned and shook her head. "I don't think so. Uncle Andrew didn't act like he knew anything. He was stunned when I told him."

Kelly smiled and shrugged his shoulders. He didn't want to push her. "You're probably right but I'd still like to find out why Anna ran away from her family. Will you help me do that?"

"Of course. I don't believe Uncle Andrew killed my mother but if he did, I wouldn't want him to get away with it. What do you want me to do?"

Krystal's voice sounded strained and Kelly squeezed her hand. "What I really want is information on your mother's past. You were just a child then, so rather than you trying to deal with this, maybe you can think of someone else who might be willing to talk to me?"

Krystal stared at him for several moments. Then she grinned. "Stella. She'd be willing enough to talk to you, if you went about it the right way."

"Your uncle's wife?"

"Being Uncle Andrew's wife doesn't bother Stella, if you know what I mean. She likes cowboys and she especially likes tall, well-built men. Do you happen to own a cowboy hat?"

Kelly laughed, then immediately choked it off. "I'm sorry but that sounded so funny coming from such a sweet little gal."

She laughed harshly. "Oh, believe me. I'm not always sweet. I know I have a blind spot where Stella's concerned. She made my childhood miserable and that affects my attitude but I'm serious about the kind of woman she is. She and Uncle Andrew stopped sharing the same bedroom years ago and she doesn't even pretend to be a faithful wife."

"Even if that's true, would she be willing to tell me things that might be damaging to your uncle?"

"I don't think she'd care. She likes damaging people. She'd probably be happy to see Uncle Andrew charged with my mother's murder because then he'd go to prison and she'd have all his money. Grandmother Davis made her sign a prenuptial agreement before she married Uncle Andrew and if she leaves him, all she gets is a monthly allowance."

"Do you think she knows anything about your mother and father? That all happened quite a while before she married your uncle, didn't it?"

"I don't know. Uncle Andrew's not the confiding type and Grandmother Davis sure wasn't. She didn't approve of Stella at all. Still,

Stella's sneaky. If there's a skeleton in our family closet, she'd have found it."

"Any suggestions about approaching Stella?"

"Oh sure, that's easy. Just tell her you're an old friend of mine who wanted to get in touch with me. When she tells you I'm away at school, act disappointed and mention you were hoping I'd show you a bit of the night life. Stella will take care of the rest."

"I'm not quite sure how to take that. Still, it might work, at least for starters. I'll eventually have to tell her who I am but maybe I can soften her up a bit before I start with the questions."

"I'm sure you can." The edge was back in her voice. Kelly winced.

"I doubt if there'll be a mutual attraction. I don't like cold, calculating women."

Krystal blushed. "I'm glad." She lowered her head until her voice was barely audible. "Because I like you."

"I like you too." Kelly smiled and brushed his fingers across the palm of her hand. "That gives me another reason to find out who killed your mother. I'd like us to get better acquainted and I don't want Anna's death hanging over our heads."

She lifted her eyes to his and they held the gaze for a long moment. Finally, Kelly took a notebook from his pocket and handed it across the table.

"Here, write down the address and phone number in Houston. Then let's forget this stuff and enjoy the rest of the evening. There's a band in the other room. Do you like to dance?"

"I love to dance."

Chapter Eleven

Kelly jerked up in the bed, tangled his arms in the sheets and grappled thin air with his hands.

"Did you bite my foot?" He glared at Jake, who basked in the early morning sunlight across the foot of the bed.

Jake hopped off the bed and stretched his legs, then opened his mouth for a big yawn and padded across to the door.

"And you don't give a damn that I didn't hit the sack until two a.m. either, do you?"

Jake shook himself and looked at Kelly.

"Nope, you don't." Kelly limbed out of bed and opened the door. "You go check out the neighborhood while I get myself together, then we'll see about some chow."

Kelly showered, dressed, made a pot of coffee and filled Jake's bowl. Cup in hand, he wandered into the living room and spotted the light blinking on his answering machine.

Kelly hit the playback button and Gus' voice boomed off the tape. "Where the hell are you? I want to talk to you about your buddy Cam. Give me a ring as soon as you can. I'll be in the office all morning."

"Shit!" Kelly swore. He'd like to kick Cam's ass himself for lying to him. And it would take some fast-talking to get Gus to approve his trip to Houston now they had Cam locked up. Best start laying the groundwork for that as soon as possible. He picked up the phone and called.

"I was beginning to think you'd eloped," Gus boomed over the wire. "That must've been some date."

"Well, I think we were the last ones left on the dance floor when the band quit for the night, anyway."

"Good for you. I guess you've heard that we picked up Cam."

"Yeah, I heard. Are you nailed down on this, Gus?"

"No, not nailed down but what we've got looks good. Why don't you meet me over at the White Bull? We'll have a cup of coffee and mull things over a bit."

"I'll catch you there."

Maybe there was hope. Gus' willingness to meet and talk was a sure sign he had a few doubts about the case. Gus might be with the Sheriff's Department now instead of the Fort Worth PD, but one thing Kelly knew about his former partner—if Gus was convinced Cam was guilty, he'd wouldn't be discussing a damn thing with Kelly, let alone setting up a meeting to do it. Maybe he'd get approval for that Houston trip after all.

It never hurt to be prepared. Kelly packed a bag for an overnight stay, gave Jake an affectionate rub and headed for Old Blue. He stopped at the bait house on the way. The sun had its high beams on and Bubba was sprawled out in a lawn chair reading a Louis L'Amour paperback and taking advantage of the warmth when Kelly hopped out of the truck.

"Hey, Kelly, what's up?"

"I'm headed for Houston. I'll probably be back early tomorrow afternoon but just in case I'm held up, how about keeping your eye on things? There's nothing going on at the flea market, so if you'll just do a walk around later tonight, that'll be good enough. Jake's got plenty of food and water but maybe after you've done the market you could stop off at the cabin and make sure everything's copacetic."

"Sure, Kelly. No problem."

"Thanks. I'll catch you later."

The White Bull on 28th Street had been a standard pit stops back in the days when Gus and Kelly were a team. Kelly slid across the cracked red plastic of the same old booth they'd always chosen. It felt good, like a homecoming.

"Just like old times." Gus's voice was muffled by the mouthful of biscuit. Kelly nodded and called the waitress over.

"I'll have the biscuits and gravy." He pointed at Gus' plate. "And throw a couple of eggs on the side." She nodded, filled his coffee cup and headed for the kitchen.

"So!" Kelly took a sip of hot coffee and looked at Gus. "You gonna tell me what's going on?"

Gus set his fork on the plate and leaned back. "Seems your friend left out a coupla' things when he told you about his run-in with Anna."

"Yeah, kinda of figured that out already. Okay, let's hear the worst."

"Cam's prints were all over that box of Anna's. So was Bubba's, but he had a reason. Or so he says. We had enough to get a warrant on Cam though. And we weren't inside his place ten minutes before we found Anna's note tucked away in the bottom drawer of his desk. That sound good to you?"

"Smartass. So what's his story?"

"About what you'd expect. He claims he went down to Anna's cabin to see if she'd come back from the flea market. Says the door was unlocked so he walked in and went to her bedroom to see if maybe she'd passed out on the bed. And then, according to his story, he spotted the box pulled out of the floor and busted wide open. Says the note was right on top and he grabbed it without thinking and got the hell out of there."

"He's probably telling the truth about that door. Most of the Creek folks leave them unlocked. Including Anna."

"Yeah, well, she may have left her door unlocked but not the box. Cam admits he went inside her cabin looking for that note. That nails him for burglary right there."

"Sure it does but you're not after a burglar, for God's sake. You're after a murderer."

"What makes you so sure we ain't got both. Two for the price of one?"

Kelly shrugged. "Call it gut instinct if you want to. And don't try and tell me that you're absolutely sure about it, either. I know you, Gus. If you were set on Cam for the big one, you wouldn't be wasting time jawing with me. You'd be out busting your ass to get your case against him nailed down. So what gives?"

"I have been busting my ass, as you so delicately put it but I admit there're a couple of things bothering me. For one thing, it's not like you to get on your high horse the way you have about this Cam character. That bothers me some. Then there's the scarf. How the hell did Cam get his hands on it? 'Cause we know he never left the Hideaway Saturday afternoon, which is when Krystal says she lost the scarf. What really bothers me though is the note. Cam admits he knew Anna's will cancelled out the note, so if he killed her, why in hell would he take the note? It just don't make sense."

"That's what I been trying to tell you. If Cam killed her, he'd have hauled ass back to the bar and built himself an alibi. Woulda' been stupid to go to her cabin and steal that note and Cam's not stupid."

"Maybe he got so damn scared after he killed her his brain wasn't working."

"I don't believe that. If Cam had committed the murder, his first thought would've been how to cover his tracks."

"Well, I'm not filing it but I'll level with you, Kelly. I'm getting a lotta pressure from upstairs and until something better comes along, Cam's just gonna have to cool his heels."

Kelly nodded. "I know all about the politics. Besides, Cam shouldn't have lied. It won't hurt him to simmer for a couple of days. Meantime, I've got an idea that might open up another line."

"What's that?"

"I asked Krystal a few questions last night and I got some interesting family background that might be worth some digging."

"Such as?"

"It seems Anna was a forbidden topic in the Davis household and not only that, no one's ever told Krystal what happened the night her father committed suicide. Still won't. That's the reason she hired a detective to track down her mother."

"I already checked that out," Gus said. "It's the same old crap. Anna ran off with a boyfriend and when her husband found out, he blew his own head off."

"I don't buy that. If it was a straightforward case of Anna being a Jezebel, why didn't they just tell Krystal all the details and let her think the worst of Anna? Nope, something's not kosher and what I'd like to do is run down to Houston and have a little chat with Krystal's Aunt Stella."

Gus rolled his eyes. "That's just what I need. You'll go on down there and start some fireworks and the next thing I know, one of Davis' hot-shot lawyers will be on the phone to the chief and I'll be up to my ass in alligators."

"That's not gonna happen." Kelly grinned and clapped his hand to his heart. "I give you my word, I won't stir up any shit. All I'll do is have a go at the aunt and see what comes out. If she balks, I'll back off and that'll be the end of it."

"I ought to have my head examined but what the hell," Gus growled. "I admit I'm not happy with some aspects of this case but my hands are tied. I'll agree to you poking around down there in Houston. As long as it's strictly unofficial. If I get any complaints, I won't know a damn thing about what you're doing."

"You got a deal." Kelly picked up the bill and headed for the front counter. "I'll get the grub."

"Don't think this evens us out from Angelo's!"

Kelly headed straight for the freeway from the café. It was one o'clock by the time he'd fought his way across Dallas and merged with I-45 to Houston. It was a four or five hours, depending on traffic and road construction, so he'd play connecting with Stella by ear. According to Krystal, Uncle Andrew often stayed at the office until nine or ten. If traffic was light, he might even see her tonight.

Luck stayed with him all the way. By five-thirty he'd reached the outskirts of Houston and merged onto the 610 Loop west and south. From there, he stayed on to the San Felipe off-ramp where he exited onto River Oaks Boulevard and whipped into a gas station to refuel. And to call the Davis residence.

"Davis residence." A woman's voice. Probably the maid or housekeeper.

"Andrew Davis, please?"

"He's not available."

Well, hell! Not available might mean anything from taking a crap to being out on the town. He'd hoped to head right over there but if Andrew was home, he'd have to wait for morning.

Kelly switched tactics. "I'm a business associate of Mr. Davis. I just got into town and I'd like to get hold of him tonight if possible."

"Have you tried the office?" The woman asked.

"No. I didn't think he'd be there this late."

"He's working on a project and isn't expected home until midnight or later."

Kelly grinned, thanked the woman for her help. He pulled the truck away from the pumps over to the side and consulted his map, looking for Pine Hill Terrace.

A ten-minute drive took him to River Oaks. He whistled low in his throat when he pulled up in front of the Davis mansion. The place was a showpiece. White-trimmed windows and casements contrasted with the red brick exterior. It shrieked of old money. Kelly climbed out of Old Blue and let himself in through the wrought iron gate.

A sleek blue Jaguar stood in front of the garage. It had to be Stella's car. Krystal had told him she drove a Jag. Kelly crossed his fingers for luck and strode up to the front door.

The hollow tone of muted chimes filtered through the heavy oak door. A few moments passed before the latch clicked and the door swung open.

The shapely redhead stepped onto the porch and arched an eyebrow. "Can I help you?" She swept her cool blue eyes down Kelly's six-foot frame.

Kelly grinned. Krystal's description hadn't quite prepared him for Stella. Her faded blue jeans fit her slim legs like a second skin and a colorful green print shirt was knotted snugly below her ample breasts.

"I hope so. I'm looking for Krystal Davis. We were at a workshop together in Austin last year and she told me to look her up if I ever made it to Houston." Stella eyed him speculatively but didn't speak. Time to go in with a big hit. "You wouldn't by any chance be her sister?"

"I'm Krystal's aunt. Krystal's living in Fort Worth."

"Oh! Well, I guess that means I'm going to be left on my lonesome." He drew out his words and kept his eyes fastened on hers. "I was hoping Krystal would show me some Houston night life."

"Too bad she's not here then." Stella smile made it clear she had an alternative.

"I don't suppose you'd care to join me for a drink?" Kelly struck while the iron was hot.

"I don't know. I'd hate Krystal to hear I'd been inhospitable to her friend but I do have a previous engagement for tonight." She paused, then flashed another smile. "Are you staying in the area?"

Kelly nodded. "The Holiday Inn over on Southwest Boulevard."

"The Longhorn Saloon's near there. If you wanted to drop by there about eleven, I could stop for a drink after my engagement."

"You're on," Kelly grinned enthusiastically. "I'll get settled in and grab a bite to eat. I'll be waiting when you get there."

Kelly smiled as he strode back to the truck. That went well. And he'd be willing to bet Stella would have a pretty good buzz going by the time she got to the Longhorn which would make it all the easier to get her talking.

Kelly registered at the hotel, dropped his bag in the room and headed for the coffee shop. He was hungry after the long drive, but a big plate of chicken-fried steak and mashed potatoes took care of that. He stopped at the front desk and asked for a ten o'clock wake-up call. He slept the minute his head hit the pillow.

The phone jangled him awake. Damn good thing he'd asked for a wakeup or he'd likely have slept through the night. That would've played hell with his plans.

He walked into the Longhorn Saloon right before eleven. It was packed. Kelly elbowed his way through the crowd and stood around watching for a table. Finally a young couple got up and he beat a short stringbean to the empty chair by a hair. Stringbean scowled and lead his chubby blonde lady away. Kelly grinned as he watched her leopard skin jacket mingle into the crowd. He waved down a waitress and ordered a longneck.

Energy pulsed through the crowd. And the band was pretty good, too. Kelly relaxed, drank his beer and waited. A cool hand fluttered against his neck.

"I see you found a table." Stella leaned over and spoke into his ear.

"Yep, and let me tell you, that took some fancy footwork." Kelly pulled out the chair beside him.

She slid into the seat and tilted her head. "Lively place, isn't it?" Oh yeah, she'd had a few drinks before arrival.

"What'll you have to drink?"

"I'll take a gin and tonic." She ran her fingers along his arm. "You know what they say about gin."

Kelly squeezed her fingers. "Good choice." He turned and gave the order to the hovering waitress.

The band swung into a two-step. Kelly reached for Stella's hand. "Wanta give it a try?" Stella nodded and followed him out to the floor. She had great rhythm and easily followed him through a series of intricate twirls.

Kelly decided to wait a while to ask questions. Over an early breakfast would be good. They danced and laughed and had several more drinks until the lights dimmed for the two o'clock closing.

"Seems a shame for the night to end. I saw a little café across the street when I came in. How 'bout some breakfast?"

Stella hooked her arm under his.

"You're on. Lead the way."

They walked in and slid into a cozy booth. After they'd given their orders, Kelly snuggled Stella up beside him.

"Wanta hear a story?"

"Your story, cowboy? 'Course I do." Stella pressed her body tighter against his.

He started in by talking about his life in Fort Worth—not too much—just the highlights.

Then he talked about Indian Creek and the Hideaway. And Anna.

She jerked away from him.

"You asshole! You set me up!"

"Now wait a minute!" He grasped her arms and turned her back to face him. "I just want to tell you about my friend and what's going on down there. All you have to do is listen. I won't press you. Sure, I'd appreciate it if you'd answer a couple of questions but it's up to you. I won't push."

Stella stared at him. Just when he was sure she was about to bolt, she settled back on the seat. And talked.

Kelly grabbed a few hours of sleep and checked out of the motel. Kelly hadn't learned anything specific but he damn sure had more pieces to play with. Gus was gonna love it. No damn wonder Uncle Andrew didn't want Krystal talking to Anna. Krystal was coming into control of her trust in a few months but she was leaving everything in Uncle Andrew's hands. But if Anna told Krystal the truth about the "other man" the night her father killed himself, she might just change her mind. And to Kelly's way of thinking, that added up to one hell of a motive for murder.

Chapter Twelve

Traffic crawled on Interstate 45. Construction had four lanes cut down to one for 50 miles and Kelly knew he never catch Gus before he left the station. By the time Kelly pulled off Jacksboro highway and headed for home, it was well past six.

Jake's tail started going full tilt when he spotted Old Blue turning into the driveway. Kelly grinned and played a tune on the horn. Even though he'd only been gone for a day, it was good to be home, good to know he'd been missed. For a long time after Lynda, there'd been no one to care if he came home, but finding Jake changed all that. Kelly wrapped his arms around Jake's neck, and collected a few licks on the chin.

They walked up the hill to the cabin. Kelly glanced at the phone. The red light flashed on the answering machine. One call from Gus and two from Krystal. He sighed, shoved his bag off the recliner and sank back into the seat. Of course Krystal wanted to know what he'd found out in Houston, but he didn't have a clue in hell how to tell her. Or what to tell her. It was a touchy situation. Kelly hated lies but this was one of those times when there didn't seem to be any options. He'd have to tell her something. Knowing her grandmother had been behind Anna running away wasn't going to come as much of a shock. The old lady was dead and she and Krystal hadn't been close. In fact, Krystal hadn't liked her much at all. What he hadn't decided was how much, if anything, to tell her about her uncle's involvement.

The telephone rang and Kelly braced himself for Krystal's voice, but it was Gus.

"Well, how'd it go down there?" Gus' voice boomed over the wire.

"Better than I expected. I tried to get back earlier so I could drop in at the station but that damn 45 was a nightmare."

"Ain't it always? Why don't you run on out here? Betty's been bugging me to bring you home and we were just talking about throwing some steaks on the grill."

"Now that's an offer I can't refuse. I was about to open a can of beans. Mind if Jake comes?"

"Hell, no. Bring him along. We'll see how he hits it off with Scooter."

Kelly hung up the phone and turned to Jake. "Well, boy, better get your butt in gear 'cause we got us an invitation to a barbecue."

172

Gus and Betty lived in a small subdivision half way between Fort Worth and Arlington. Kelly hit the tail end of rush hour. Memories flooded his mind as he picked his way through traffic. He and Lynda had been frequent visitors to the neat little rambler where Gus and Betty had raised three kids and an assortment of dogs, cats and rabbits. Kelly swallowed a large lump when he pulled into the familiar driveway. It never went away. He reached over and opened the passenger door. Jake jumped to the ground and perked his ears toward the house. Betty must have heard the truck from the kitchen because she was standing on the front porch waving both hands and smiling the big, warm smile Kelly remembered so well.

"Land sakes, boy." She met him at the foot of the steps and reached her chubby arms around his neck so she could plant a big kiss on his cheek. "I was convinced you'd up and died on us, until Gus came home and told me he'd found you hiding out down there at Indian Creek."

"I've missed you, Betty."

She smiled up into his eyes, blinking a bit to keep back tears. "You get yourself into the house and tell that big lug of mine to dig you a cold one outta the fridge."

"It's good to see you, Betty." Kelly pulled her back for another hug. "It's been too darn long."

She tilted her head and gave him a sharp look. "Now you're back and I'll expect to see you around real often." Her eyes shone with affection and Kelly choked back another lump.

"This place gets darn lonesome now that the last of the young'uns has gone off and got herself hitched," Betty said. Then, mindful of the emotions gripping them both, she shook her dishtowel and herded him toward the door. "Off with you now. Gus is in the study. I've got to get back to the kitchen. There's a pan of that jalapeno corn bread you always liked so well browning in the oven and I don't want it burnt to a crisp."

Jake, who had hung back during this exchange, climbed the steps and joined them at the door.

"Who's this you've got with you?" Betty bent down and held out her hand for Jake to sniff.

"Jake, meet Betty," Kelly said. "She's the best cook in the State of Texas, so you'd better get on her good side."

"You go on in there too, boy," Betty said. "Four-legged critters is as welcome as two-legged ones in this old house."

Kelly headed straight for the study where he found Gus stretched out in the same well-worn leather recliner he'd had for as long as Kelly could remember.

"I got you all fixed up." Gus pointed to the can of Budweiser stuck in a Koozie and setting on the whatnot table beside Betty's old armchair.

Kelly sank down in the soft cushion, raised his long legs up on the flower print footstool Betty always kept parked in front of her chair and let out a deep sigh.

Jake carefully sniffed the room and then padded over to a throw rug in front of the patio doors. He eased himself down on his haunches.

Gus laughed. "Smart dog. He's scented Scooter right off. Hey, Scoot! Get your butt down here."

A thumping scuffle echoed along the hallway and moments later, a black-and-white cocker spaniel skidded into the room and slid to a halt in front of Gus.

Jake's ears perked forward and the muscles rippled along his haunches.

"Go on over there and join our guest." Gus pointed to Jake.

Scooter padded across the room, sniffed the edge of the rug and parked himself nose-to-nose with Jake.

Gus chuckled as the two dogs eyed each other warily. "They'll get acquainted. Now, let's hear what you've been up to. I hope I don't find myself ass deep in alligators come Monday morning."

Kelly laughed. "Nope. I didn't even ripple the pond while I was down there. Matter of fact, I had the luck of the Irish riding with me the whole trip. I ran down Krystal's Aunt Stella the first night and let me tell you, that woman's a pistol. We met over at the Longhorn Saloon and dusted up the floor for a couple of hours. And after we quit the club, I took her out for some grub and told her why I'd come to town."

"You told her the truth?"

"Yep!" Kelly grinned at Gus' surprised expression. "It just seemed like the right thing to do. Of course, it was touch and go at first as to whether or not she was going to walk out and leave me wishing I'd kept my mouth shut but she came around in the end and boy, did she give me an earful."

"Well, don't keep me waiting. What did she have to say?"

Kelly grinned and picked up his beer can. Gus glared at him while he took a long swallow and then set the can back on the table. "For starters," Kelly said, "I found out why Anna dropped out of sight. It seems the other man in Anna's life was none other than Krystal's Uncle Andrew."

Gus frowned. "No wonder he's been scrambling to keep us from digging too deep into Anna's past."

"Yep. The family kept the lid on the story for years. Even Stella didn't know what happened until Vivian Davis developed Alzheimer's. Vivian never liked Stella but as the disease progressed, Stella took on her personal care and Vivian began treating her like a confidant. Then, during one of her memory lapses, she started talking about Anna. Stella urged her along and Vivian told her the whole story."

"So what's the story?"

"In a nutshell, Clayton came home early from a business trip and caught Anna and Andrew in bed together. It seems the shock was more than Clayton could handle. He walked out of the bedroom and went straight downstairs to the study and blew his brains out."

"That checks with the suicide story." Gus said, nodding his head.

"Anna and Andrew heard the shot from the bedroom and raced downstairs. As soon as they realized Clayton was dead, Andrew took off for his mother's house. Vivian lived just a couple houses from Anna and Clayton. When Andrew told her what had happened, she told him to stay at her house while she went over to Clayton's and dealt with Anna."

"Kind of strange behavior for a mother, wouldn't you say? Telling Andrew to stay at the house when her oldest boy's just killed himself?"

Kelly shrugged. "Don't think Vivian was exactly your normal kind of mother. Once Andrew told her Clayton was dead, looks like she decided it was more important to protect the son she had than mourn the one she'd lost."

"Sounds that way. What was Anna doing while Andrew was chasing off after his mother?"

"Pretty much sitting there in shock. Vivian told Stella when she got to the house, she found Anna crouched over Clayton's body holding the gun."

"Oh, ho!" Gus' eyes lit up. "So that's where this is going."

"Oh, yeah. My guess is soon as the old lady realized Clayton was dead, she knew she had her golden opportunity. Stella says Vivian laughed like a madwoman when she told her how she got rid of 'that hussy'."

"So how'd she work it?"

Kelly shrugged. "Just like you think. Ultimatum style. Either Anna signed everything over to daughter Krystal with Andrew as guardian and get the hell out of Dodge, or

Vivian'd make sure she went to the gas chamber for murdering Clayton."

"Even though Anna was with Andrew when Clayton shot himself?"

"Andrew'd swear to anything his mother said and Anna knew it just as well as Vivian did. And besides, what with the circumstances of Clayton's death, she probably believed she was guilty, at least morally, if not legally. The Anna I knew would. I doubt if she even tried to fight the old lady at that point and later, even if she wanted to change her mind, well, it was just too late."

"Leaving Andrew in control of everything until Krystal came of age."

"Exactly! But Krystal's turning twenty-five in a couple of months and that's when Andrew's guardianship is scheduled to end."

"Then if Andrew's about to lose control anyhow, not much benefit to him from killing Anna."

"Oh, but there would be. Krystal told me she doesn't have any interest at all in getting involved with either the business or her own estate. She's already told Andrew she's perfectly content to let him manage them both and from what I understand, she's planning on signing an agreement extending the trust when she does turn twenty-five."

"I'll be damned." Gus whistled. "Come to Papa."

"Exactly. All Andrew had to do was keep Krystal away from Anna for another two months and he'd have been set for life. I figure he must've damn near had a coronary when he got the call from Jack Boscon saying he'd been hired by Krystal to locate her mother and the two of them were meeting that weekend."

"So the next question is where the hell was Andrew Davis last Saturday night?"

"You read my mind." Kelly grinned and reached for his beer. "I kind of figured maybe you'd get on the horn to Houston come Monday morning."

"Monday, hell. I'll give them a call first thing in the morning. I wasn't exactly anxious to stir up a hornet's nest with the Davises based on what we had. But this shit changes things."

"So where does that leave Cam?"

"For now, right where he's sitting. Old Bill's been screaming his head off for us to either charge him or let him loose. So the DA's decided to charge him with burglary. And I need Cam locked up to keep the heat off until I've had a chance to look into this Davis angle."

Kelly nodded. "I understand but Cam's got his whole life wrapped up in that bar of his. If you nail him on a burglary rap, the TABC will yank his liquor license. You might as well fry him as take the Hideaway away from him."

"I know that but like I said, I can't do anything else right now. But if your friend, Cam, didn't murder the old gal and we catch the killer, I'll go to the DA and recommend he drop the burglary charges. And if you tell anybody I said that, I'll call you a liar."

"Thanks, Gus. 'Cause I'd bet Old Blue against that broken down recliner of yours Cam's innocent."

"Okay, that's settled. I'll call Houston in the morning and pass it by Captain Jeffrey. If he gives me the go ahead, I just might take a little trip down there myself. Now let's get those steaks on the grill before Betty comes out here and pins our ears back."

The rest of the night was a trip down memory lane for Kelly. Some of it was painful, especially when he wandered into the living room and saw his and Lynda's wedding picture still sitting in the same spot Betty'd put it fifteen years ago.

Mostly though, he thoroughly enjoyed himself. There was nothing like being with old friends to give him the feeling of having a special place in the human race and the Grahams were more than friends. Kelly hadn't had any contact with his dad in over twenty-five years and his mom had died the year after he and Lynda were married. Gus and Betty were all the family he had besides Jake.

It was eleven-thirty when Kelly got home. He didn't intend to call Krystal until morning but the light was flashing on his answering machine and when he punched the button, she pleaded with him from the tape.

"Kelly, this is Krystal. I hope you don't think I'm being a pest but I can't stand the suspense. Did you get in touch with Stella? Call me, please. I don't care what time it is. I won't sleep anyhow for wondering about you."

Kelly smiled and picked up the telephone. Lynda had been like that. She couldn't stand waiting.

The phone only rang once.

"Hello!"

"Hello, yourself. I got your message, so I took you at your word about being awake. I'm sorry to be so late getting back to you but I've just now come from Gus' place."

"I'm so glad you called. I've been holding my breath ever since you left."

"Well, you better breathe then." Kelly chuckled. "To answer your question—yes, I did get in touch with Stella. I met her over at the Longhorn Saloon, we danced a bit and I took her out for breakfast. You were right. She was friendly and she answered most of my questions."

"Oh!" She inhaled sharply. "Are you going to tell me what she said?"

"Sure." Kelly crossed his fingers. "Most of it won't be any news to you and there isn't anything to keep you from getting a good night's sleep. How 'bout I take you out for dinner tomorrow night and talk about it then?"

"How 'bout you come for dinner here? Penny's a terrific cook and she's already asked me to invite you over for dinner one night. So tomorrow? She's very tactful, so after dinner I know she'll find something to do so we can talk."

"Sounds like a winner to me. What time?"

"Five o'clock? That'll give Penny plenty of time."

"Great. I'll be looking forward to it."

Kelly was up at daybreak Saturday morning. Saturday and Sunday were business days at the flea market and it was part of Kelly's job to make sure all the day-jobbers were set up in the right section. They kept him hopping all morning. It was noon before he got a break and went to the cabin for lunch. He checked the flashing light on the answering machine. Gus. Kelly threw a couple of frozen burritos into the microwave and dialed Gus' home number.

"What's up?"

"Remember the license number you got from that anonymous caller?"

"Sure. What about it?"

"You aren't gonna believe this one."

"Don't tell me it's turned out that jerk was on the level."

"Oh, the guy was on the level all right. The only problem was, he needed an eye exam. The number he gave us was LQY-464. Which belonged to a fella named Donovan Nolan. We checked Nolan out good and after he came out clean, we wrote your caller off as a crank."

"I remember. So Nolan's not so clean after all?"

"Oh no, Nolan's out of it. And it's just damn luck and your trip to Houston that turned this up. See, after what you told me about Andrew Davis, I went ahead and did a background check. Which naturally included his vehicle registrations and plate numbers. Nearly split a gut when the number on his BMW turned out to be LQV-464."

"You're putting me on."

"Nope, I'm giving it to you straight. And I still haven't told you the best part."

"You mean there's more?"

"Yep. Once I had the number, I ran it through our local computer. Just on the off chance a man in a hurry might have a heavy foot. And I hit the jackpot, 'cause he did. One of our units wrote Andrew Davis a citation for doing sixty-five in a fifty and you'll never guess where and when."

"Not in the vicinity? We're not that lucky."

"Oh, son! He was logged in two miles the other side of Lake Country Estates at one forty-nine on Sunday morning."

"Jackpot!"

"Yessir. I've already booked a flight to Houston. Mr. Davis and I, we're going to have us a nice, long chat."

"Poor Krystal. It'll hit her pretty hard if it turns out he's the one."

"Yeah, but if he's a killer, she can consider herself lucky. Murderers have a habit of repeating and that little gal's got too damn much money for her own good."

"I'm having dinner with her tonight. It's going to be tough trying to act like I don't know anything's going down."

"Just be careful what you say. I know you've gotten close but you don't really know how things stand between her and her uncle."

"That goes without saying, Gus. As far as I'm concerned, we didn't even have this conversation and I wasn't about to tell Krystal anything about her uncle anyhow. She wants some answers but I figured I'd just focus on the grandmother. She didn't like her grandmother much anyhow. Even if Andrew turns out to be the murderer, there's still a chance the story about him and Anna will never come out."

"Okay. I'll give you a call as soon as I get back from Houston. By the way, Cam posted bail on the burglary charge. He ought to be home sometime this afternoon."

"Good. Thanks, Gus. At least this is a break for Cam, even if it does turn out to be pretty tough on Krystal."

Kelly finished up at the flea market by three-thirty, giving him plenty of time to spruce up for his dinner date. He chose a light blue shirt topped off with a dark blue vest. Lynda always told him blues made his eyes look sexy. He kind of hoped Krystal would have the same reaction.

Dressed and ready, he grabbed the bouquet of crimson dahlias and pink roses he'd picked up from Loretta Carter's flower stand and headed for Old Blue. Inside the pickup, he propped the flowers against the passenger door and leaned out the window.

"You watch the place," he called to Jake before he wheeled out of the garage and headed for town.

Krystal took his breath away when she met him at the door. Her silvery blond hair danced over her shoulders in soft waves framing her sun-kissed face. Her mint green pullover hugged her breasts and a chain of gold coins accented her tiny waist. Kelly whistled his admiration.

"Thank you," she said, dipping him a little curtsy. "What lovely flowers."

"Fitting, I'd say, for two such beautiful hostesses." Kelly handed Krystal the flowers and smiled over her shoulder at Penny, peeking her head around the kitchen doorway.

"How are you, Penny?"

"Very good. I hope you brought appetite. Maybe too much food."

"I'll bet I can put a good dent in it." Kelly sniffed the air. "I'm starved and it sure smells good in here."

"Chinese. You like?"

"My mouth's watering already."

Krystal took the flowers and arranged them in a large cut glass vase. She pointed toward the small living room. "Let's sit in here while Penny finishes dinner."

Kelly nodded and followed her down the hall. Inside, he had his choice between the armchair Gus had chosen when he questioned the girls or a cozy love seat. Smiling at Krystal, he walked over to the love seat. She followed, smiled into his eyes and sat down beside him.

"I'm glad you came."

"How could I resist being entertained by two beautiful women and from what my nose tells me, a scrumptious meal to boot?"

"I hope you don't think I'm lazy, letting Penny do all the work. I tried to help her but she shooed me out of the kitchen. I'm a terrible cook."

"I doubt if you have much to worry about. Any man with a lick of sense would be satisfied to have you sit around and look beautiful all day."

Krystal laughed and leaned her head back, letting it rest in the curve of his shoulder. "I suppose you're not going to tell me anything until after dinner."

"Of course not. You can't expect a hungry man to carry on a conversation, can you?"

Penny appeared in the doorway and smiled at the two of them snuggled up together on the love seat. "We eat now," she said. They rose to join her in the kitchen.

The table, covered with a yellow cloth and set with red brick stoneware, had the festive air of a party. They took their seats and Penny carried in a tray stacked with four steaming bowls.

"Wow!" Kelly's eyes gleamed. "From the looks of it, you cooked enough to feed an army. Look out, though. As good as it smells, Penny, there might not be much left when I push away from the table. What have you got here?"

Penny beamed. "This one is beef with oyster sauce." She indicated a bowl filled with thick chunks of beef and mushrooms, sprinkled with sesame seeds. "The other two are shrimp dishes. The shrimp in chili sauce has much spice. Krissie say you like hot food."

"Mmmm, you bet I do. What's this?" He pointed to a bowl filled with thick patties covered with chunks of pineapple and mandarin oranges.

"That is sweet and sour pork."

"Well, if it tastes anything like it smells, you're gonna have to fight me for leftovers."

The food was wonderful. The three of them laughed and joked through the meal and read laughed louder as they read each other's fortunes from the fortune cookies Penny served with tea as dessert. When the meal was done, Penny started to clear the table and Kelly grasped her wrist. "Hold it, little gal. You've just finished feeding me like a king. I'll do the clean-up. Anyway, I need the exercise after a meal like that."

"He's right." Krystal jumped up and placed her hands on Penny's shoulders. "You scoot into the living room and relax while Kelly and I clean up."

"Okay, okay." Penny laughed and put up her hands. "Adelle wants me to come, watch television. I go then. Okay?"

"Of course." Krystal smiled at her roommate's gracious withdrawal.

"I told you she was tactful," she said after Penny had left the room.

"Yeah and a great cook too. What's your preference—washing or drying?"

"Oh, I'll just rinse them and stick them in the dishwasher. You can carry them into the kitchen for me if you'd like."

"You got it." Kelly grabbed a couple of bowls. "Lead the way."

"This is tough." Kelly said after they had finished the dishes and were back on the love seat. "I'm going to have to tell you some things about your grandmother you might not like. Are you sure you want to hear them?"

"Of course I'm sure. I've been trying to find out what happened between my parents ever since I was a little girl. Besides, my grandmother and I weren't close. I didn't like her much and nothing she did would surprise me."

"Well, you'll have to use your own judgment on how much of this you want to accept as gospel. Stella was only able to repeat what she heard from your grandmother before she died and I guess she wasn't too lucid."

"No, she wasn't. She died two years ago and I was already living here in Fort Worth. I didn't see much of her in the year before she died but the last time I went home, she didn't even know who I was."

"Okay." Kelly smiled and squeezed her hand. "According to Stella, your father caught Anna in bed with another man and that's why he killed himself. Anna found your father's body in the study and called your grandmother. It seems Vivian decided to use your father's death as a means to get rid of Anna and get Andrew made your custodian so she could direct your life."

"I don't know why she wanted me." Krystal's eyes were bright. "She never liked me. She was always telling me I was just like my mother and she made it pretty obvious what she thought of her."

"I'm sorry." Kelly stroked her cheek and pulled her against his chest.

"It's okay. I already knew my mother was unfaithful to my father. Uncle Andrew told me that much. I can't figure out how my grandmother used Daddy's death to send her away, though."

"Anna was hysterical when she found your father's body and she picked up the gun. She was still holding it in her hand when your grandmother walked in. She threatened to tell the police Anna murdered your father unless Anna gave Andrew custody and agreed to let him take over the business until you were old enough to inherit."

"And my mother agreed to that." Krystal shook her head in disbelief.

"She didn't have much choice in the matter. Your grandmother was prepared to swear she arrived at the house and found your mother standing over your father's body with a gun in her hand. In other words, she either had to leave town without you or be charged with murder."

Krystal rubbed her eyes and tried to wipe out the tears. Kelly reached over and tugged her into his lap.

"It's all right," he said. "You go ahead and cry. I know this hurts like hell but maybe now that you know the truth, you can put it in the past and get on with your own life."

Kelly rocked her gently back and forth while she sobbed against his chest.

Finally, her breathing slowed and she lifted her head. "I'm sorry," she said getting to her feet. "I'll be right back. I need to wash my face. Don't worry. I'm okay."

Kelly sighed and watched her walk stiffly out of the room. He'd hated to do that but he'd been afraid not to. If it turned out Andrew was Anna's murderer, Krystal was really going to be hit between the eyes.

"I'm a mess." Krystal smiled weakly when she came back into the room. Her eyes were puffy and her cheeks were flushed but she definitely wasn't what Kelly would call a mess.

"You're beautiful." He swallowed the lump in his throat. "I'm sorry I had to hurt you like that."

"You didn't hurt me. They did. I've always known what my grandmother was like. It was just the shock of hearing about it that hit me so hard. I'm okay now. Really I am. There's one thing I would like to know, though. Did Stella tell you who the man was that my mother ran away with?"

"No." Kelly's eyebrow twitched when he spoke. "I don't think she knew."

"I guess it doesn't matter anyhow. It's all in the past. I just wondered if he might have had something to do with my mother's death."

"I doubt it. At least I've never seen Anna with anyone but Bubba and I've been right there for the last five years."

"What about my uncle? You don't still think he murdered my mother, do you? I can see him trying to keep me from finding out what my grandmother did to my mother but he wouldn't have any reason to kill her."

"I honestly don't know who killed Anna but I do think your uncle might know something he's not telling."

"But Uncle Andrew didn't even know where my mother was."

"Didn't he?"

"You mean you think he did." Krystal narrowed her eyes.

"I didn't say that, Krystal. I just meant there are a lot of questions that still haven't been answered. I'm sure the police are going to find out exactly where everybody who knew Anna was on the night of the murder."

"What about that Bubba? Maybe he thought he was going to inherit my mother's money."

"No." Kelly shook his head. "Bubba knew Anna had a daughter."

"How do you know that?"

"Because he told me he did."

"I'm sorry." Krystal touched his hand. "I didn't mean to accuse him. I know he's your friend. It's just—everything's so ugly. I don't know what to think."

"I know." Kelly smiled and squeezed her hand. "How about if we change the subject?"

She nodded and a gleam of mischief showed in her eyes. "By the way, how did you get Stella to tell you all this?"

"Not the way you're thinking." He laughed and pulled her closer. "Actually, I told her the truth about me being a friend of Cam's and trying to investigate Anna's death. We hit it off pretty well and I think she just decided to be frank with me. She's not such a bad sort, you know. She just tries to act like a hard case."

"You would think that. You're a man." She snapped the words and her eyes flashed.

"Okay!" Kelly threw up his hands. "I think I'll leave that alone."

Krystal snuggled against his chest and he placed his fingers under her chin and turned up her face. "Would it seem like I was taking advantage of the situation if I was to kiss you?"

"No, I don't think it would seem like that," she said. Her eyes sparkled as she leaned toward him.

His lips sought her mouth and she met him with a passion that surprised and stirred him. "I wanted to do that the other night," he whispered into her ear, "but I was afraid it might scare you away."

"I'm not scared." Her breath tickled his neck as she spoke. "I wanted it too. Do you mind if I ask you something very personal?"

"I guess you'll have to ask me before I can answer that, won't you?"

"Would you tell me what happened to your wife?"

Kelly stiffened. The question caught him off guard and a flash of anger showed in his eyes.

She reached out and grasped his hand.

"Don't get mad," she pleaded. "I'm not just prying. I really care about you, Kelly. I could feel your hurt when you talked about her. I've shared so much of my life with you I guess I hoped you'd be willing to share a bit of yourself."

"I'm not mad." Kelly tightened his hand on her fingers. "You just caught me by surprise. You're right, though. I think both you and I know there's some chemistry going on between us and it's only fair you should know where I'm coming from."

Krystal lifted his hand and brushed his finger with her lips. "I guess that's why I've been wondering about your wife."

Kelly took a deep breath. "Lynda died five years ago. I was on the police force working undercover narcotics. I'd infiltrated one of the biker gangs."

"That's how come you're such good friends with Detective Graham?"

"That's right. Gus used to be my partner. I've known him all my life." Kelly paused for a moment. "I won't go into all the details—just the bare facts, okay?"

"Of course but you don't have to tell me. I'll understand if it's too painful."

"No, I want to. You and I are talking about having a relationship together and you've got a right to know about Lynda. It's just that her death was so devastating, I still have a hard time talking about it."

Krystal nodded and rested her head against his shoulder.

In a low, quiet voice Kelly told her about the bikers, about Lynda being trapped in the fire, about his own feelings of guilt and about the agony of loss that had plagued him ever since.

Krystal lay in his arms, her fingers gripping his hand and when he finished, she put her lips to his mouth.

Kelly was weak from the release of pent-up emotions and the warmth of her breasts pressing tightly against his chest aroused him. He tightened his arms around her back and she came to him, molding her body against his, inviting his response. His eyes met hers with a question and in answer, she grasped his hands and placed them under her sweater.

He stroked her soft flesh, sought the hooks of her bra, released it and gently explored her nipples. She squirmed beneath his hands, grasped the sweater and pulled it off. He closed his eyes and with a soft moan, she leaned over him and pressed her nipple against his lips. His tongue explored the hard peak and his hands grasped her buttocks and pressed her against his groin. She moaned louder and reached for his zipper, freeing his organ from the confines of blue jeans. Stroking him, she set his blood to boiling.

"I love the way you touch me," she said, moving her lips against his.

"Do you want to go on?" He groaned and lifted his head to search her eyes.

She nodded and a gentle flush spread across her cheeks as she reached into her pocket and took out a small package. He smiled, relieved to realize she'd thought about this beforehand. He wouldn't have wanted her to regret their passion.

Tearing open the wrapper, Kelly prepared himself and lay back on the couch.

Keeping her eyes locked on his, Krystal stood over him and slowly removed the rest of her clothing.

"God, you're beautiful," Kelly said when she dropped her panties on the floor and lowered herself into his waiting arms.

Smiling, she straddled his waist and reached for his hardness. Stroking it gently, she drew him inside the soft, moist center of her womanhood.

Grasping each other, they merged as one, spinning into a whirlwind, giving and taking greedily as they met each other's need. Finally, sweating and spent, they collapsed against the sofa.

"That was so special," Kelly whispered against her ear.

"For me too," she said, in the husky voice of fulfillment.

For several minutes, they lay still holding each other and when they finally sat up, Kelly snuggled her into his arms.

"I hate to leave now," he said. "But I've got to make rounds at the flea market."

She smiled, happiness shining from her eyes. "Of course you've got to go. It was wonderful, Kelly. Come on, I'll walk you to your truck."

He drew her to him one more time and caressed her lips. "Before I go, I'm going to tell you something I probably shouldn't. It means betraying a confidence and I hate that but I just can't walk out of here and leave you unprepared for what might happen on Monday."

"What's going to happen?" Her eyes widened with sudden fear.

"Gus found out that your uncle was in town the night Anna was murdered. He's going to Houston to question him."

Krystal's forehead creased in a puzzled frown. "Uncle Andrew was here? I don't understand. He never said anything about having been in Fort Worth."

Kelly shook his head. "I can't give you any details. That wouldn't be fair to Gus but I just wanted to warn you your uncle might be more involved than he's led you to believe. I'm going out on a limb talking to you, so please don't repeat any of this to your uncle."

"Of course not. I don't know what Uncle Andrew could've been doing in Fort Worth but I doubt if he'd tell me even if I asked him."

Chapter Thirteen

It was just past eight when Kelly made it back to Indian Creek. There were several vehicles parked around the bait house and down by the creek. Frank Perkins stood in the center of a group of men. Kelly pulled into the driveway and joined Marty Jenkins on the edge of the group.

"What's all the excitement?" he asked.

"That's Frank's new boat." Marty pointed to a gleaming new bass boat fastened to the end of the dock. "Isn't she a honey?"

"She's a stunner all right."

From inside the circle of men, Frank's high, excited voice carried to where Kelly stood. "She's a sixteen footer with a hundred-and-fifty horsepower motor," Frank said, his face gleamed with pride. "See that gadget up on the console?" He pointed so the admiring circle of listeners could identify the object. "That's an electronic fish finder."

"Damn!" Doug Phillips piped in. "Won't be no need for you to go fishing, Frank. Y'all can just send that boat along and it'll catch 'em for yuh."

"That isn't as farfetched as you might think." Frank puffed out his chest. "All I gotta do is turn that gadget on and it'll spot every damn fish in the lake."

Doug tipped back his cap and scratched his head. "I'll be danged," he said. "What won't they think of next?"

"Hey, Frank." Kelly moved closer to the group and broke into the conversation. "What did you do? Win the state lottery?"

"Nah. My sister out in California died last year and the lawyers just now sent me my share of the estate."

"Oh! Sorry she passed away but it's nice she remembered you in her will."

"Yeah...well...I had it coming to me." Frank's round face flushed with color. "She got the house and property out in California when my old man died, so it's only right I should get my share back. As it is, I didn't get all I should've. She left most of it to that good-for-nothing kid of hers."

Kelly regretted asking any questions at all. "Well, nice to see you got yourself a new boat anyhow."

"I ain't getting any younger," Frank growled. "'Bout damn time I got some of the things I been wanting."

Kelly nodded and strolled back to Marty.

"Have you heard what's going on with Cam?" Marty asked.

"That's where I was headed when I stopped off here to see what all the excitement was about," Kelly said.

"You think the cops are gonna charge him with Anna's murder?"

"You'd have to ask Cam about that." Kelly smiled to take the sting out of his words. Marty was a good guy but like all the old timers at the Creek, he liked to gossip and Kelly wasn't about to feed the rumor mill.

"Guess I'll catch you later," he said, starting toward his truck. "I want to stop by and see Cam before I make my rounds at the flea market."

"See you later." Several voices called and Kelly lifted his hand in farewell.

When Kelly entered the Hideaway after his inspection of the flea market, Cam was sitting on a stool behind the bar with a towel in his hand and a frosted mug perched on the coaster in front of him. Marty and Leroy argued over their cribbage game at the back table and Darlene bent over the sink washing mugs. They were all in exactly the same spot they'd been in a week ago before a murderer struck and turned their lives upside down.

"You don't look any the worse for wear." Kelly pulled up a stool and held out a hand to Cam.

"Looks are deceiving," Cam returned Kelly's handshake.

"So, now that we've got the amenities out of the way," Kelly lifted his left eyebrow and gave Cam his best glare, "what the hell is all this bullshit about you busting into Anna's cabin?"

Cam's jaw dropped and a red flush spread up his face. "Hey, I'm sorry about that, Kelly. I know I should've told you but I was afraid you'd think I killed Anna if you found out I swiped the note." Cam wiped the back of his neck with the bar towel and stood there looking sheepish.

"Oh, yeah, you got no idea how much I appreciated having Gus drop that bit of news on me. If I hadn't already talked to Bubba and figured out you'd probably been down to Anna's cabin that night, I'd have looked like a damn fool."

"Yeah. That was a stupid move on my part. What can I say? I'm sorry."

"Okay. We'll let it drop. I just hope you haven't held back anything else. And if you did, then for God's sake, tell me now."

"I haven't, Kelly. I swear it. One thing you gotta believe, though. I didn't break into Anna's box. I admit I went to her cabin looking for the note but the door was open when I got there and that damn box was busted open and lying on the bed."

"Are you saying somebody else was there before you?"

"That's right." Cam got up and filled his mug, then leaned back across the bar. "I wasn't going to keep that note, you know. I just wanted to hold onto it until I had a chance to talk to Anna after she'd sobered up a bit. Then, when I realized the money was gone, I didn't know what the hell to do."

"What money are you talking about?"

"The twenty thousand dollars Anna got from the bank for the down payment on that fish camp. I took her to Fort Worth Friday and she drew it out of her savings account."

Kelly slapped his hand against his forehead. "What the hell happened to the 'oh, no, there's nothing I ain't told you'? And where in the hell you been keeping your brain lately? It never occurred to you that the money might be the motive for Anna's murder?"

"I know I should've told you but everything happened so damn fast. Besides, I thought Bubba'd tell you. Anna was getting the money for him, you know. I figured if he told you the money was missing, I could just stay out of it. It seemed like the best idea at the time."

"Bubba never said shit. Hell, he probably figured you took the money and he didn't want to rat on a friend. Damn you guys and your misplaced sense of loyalty. How the hell am I supposed to help you if you keep holding out on me?"

Cam hung his head and Kelly could tell that he'd hurt his feeling.

"Okay." Kelly struggled to keep the irritation out of his voice. "I can understand why you might keep it to yourself at first but what about later—once the cops questioned you? Didn't it occur to you then that Bubba hadn't said anything about the money? Why didn't you give me a call and tell me about it after they locked you up?"

"I was going to. I even thought about calling you from the jail but then I decided I'd better wait 'til I got out. You know cops… I've heard they bug them telephones."

"You watch too damn much television. I'm sure as hell going to have to tell Gus about this and he isn't going to like it when he finds out you been holding out on him."

"Damn it, Kelly. You go telling him about the money and where the hell does that leave me?"

"It'll leave you in a helluva lot better spot than you'll be in if he finds out on his own. I wasn't going to tell you this yet but Gus already told me if you aren't involved in the murder, he'll ask the DA to drop the burglary charges against you."

Cam's eyes widened. "You ain't kidding? He really agreed to do that?"

"Yeah, provided you're clean on the murder. But he might have changed his mind about that he's found out about that missing money. He hasn't mentioned it to me but he knows you and I are tight, so he probably wouldn't. But I'll tell you one thing, though. Gus is too damn thorough when he makes an investigation not to have found out Anna withdrew a large sum of money from her account on Friday. And for damn sure, he's probably already found a witness who'll testify you took Anna to the bank."

"I never thought about that. Why do you suppose he hasn't questioned me about the money if he already knows?"

"Because right now he's investigating a murder, not a robbery. He's probably gathered up a whole bunch of shit he hasn't seen fit to share with you or me either but you can bet your ass he'll bring it up when the time is right."

"What do you think I oughta do?"

"Nothing. Just sit tight and keep your mouth shut. I want to have a few words with Bubba, then I'll go see Gus and tell him about the money. You keep your mouth shut about all this. Don't you be discussing Anna at all, not even with Darlene."

"Ain't been talking about it anyhow. To tell you the truth, I'm sick to death of the whole damn thing. I'm sorry as hell Anna's dead but I can't help her none now and I just wish this whole pile of shit would go away and let me get back to running my business."

"I know, it's tough on everybody. I'll do some thinking about the money angle and see what I can come up with. If Gus wants to talk to you, he'll let you know, otherwise just keep your head and try to get things back to normal around here. I'll keep in touch and let you know if anything develops."

On the way to the flea market, Kelly replayed his conversation with Frank. The little weasel had been plenty evasive when Kelly started questioning him about his sister's inheritance and it was one hell of a coincidence his coming up with that inheritance at exactly the same time a bunch of money turned up missing out of Anna's strongbox.

By the time Kelly got to the flea market, it was almost nine. For the next hour and a half he was too busy to indulge in any more speculation about Frank's sudden wealth. Most of the dealers had shut down and Kelly was kept hopping retrieving tables and issuing gate cards for Sunday's business. He bolted the door when he finished and whistled for Jake, who'd been taking a run around the grounds.

"I don't know about you," Kelly said when the dog joined him on the path, "but I'm ready to call it a night."

At the cabin, Kelly grabbed a couple of hotdogs out of the fridge and tossed them in the microwave. He gave Jake one and took the other over to his recliner to stretch out and think about Frank's inheritance. Pretty big coincidence, Frank getting his money at the same time as Anna's twenty thousand dollars disappeared. And more than strange Frank hadn't mentioned the anticipated windfall before. Keeping his mouth shut simply wasn't in his make-up. No way he hadn't had notification about the estate before the money was distributed.

So why hadn't he bragged about it all over Indian Creek? The only reason for secrecy Kelly could think of was if the money had come from Anna's lock box and not an inheritance. What was Frank really doing at the creek the night Anna and Cam had their fight? Was he really night fishing? Or had he just come from rifling Anna's cabin?

Kelly got up and un-cramped his legs. Before he got anymore worked up about Frank, he needed to check out his story. The Hideaway was still open and Darlene had been quite friendly with Frank's sister when she'd visited a couple of years ago. Maybe she knew her last name and where she lived. That should give Kelly enough to call Jim Forbes in Dallas. Jim's brother was a probate lawyer in Los Angeles and should be able to check out the details of the sister's estate. He laughed. All that was called working the good old boy network and it was one of the most effective investigative tools ever created.

Kelly dialed the Hideaway, got Cam and asked if he could speak with Darlene.

"Sure, hold on a sec, I'll get her."

"How you doing, gal?" Kelly said, when Darlene's voice came on the line.

"Just fine, Kelly. What's up?"

"Oh, nothing much. I just wondered if you happened to remember Frank's sister's last name and where she lived."

"Sure. Her name was Perkins, same as Frank. She changed back to her maiden name when she and her old man got divorced. She lived in San Clemente but she died last year, you know."

"Yeah, I knew that but I needed to get some information about her and listen, I'd appreciate it if you'd keep this under your hat, okay?"

"Sure, no problem. I wouldn't have any reason to talk about it, anyhow."

"Thanks. You're a gem. Talk to you later."

Kelly replaced the receiver. "Well, that was simple." Darlene was good about keeping her mouth shut, so he needn't worry on that account.

The next thing was to get hold of Jim and that was something he needed to do anyhow. It'd been six months since they'd talked. Jim understood the reason Kelly seldom saw him. Kelly'd been at Jim's house the night Lynda died, the night Kelly's world had ended in flames. He had a hard time dealing with his own guilt whenever he spent any time around Jim. That wasn't Jim's fault and Kelly needed to put things right between them. Jim liked to fish. He'd probably jump at the chance to spend a weekend here at Indian Creek.

"Hey, buddy, how you doin?" Kelly said when Jim's cheerful voice came over the line.

"Kelly! I'm great. Good to hear from you. What's going on with you? You still buried out there in the boonies?"

Kelly laughed. "Yep, still a creek rat. I figured you'd still be up, knowing how you like to burn the midnight oil."

"It's the only time the place is quiet enough to sort out my own thoughts. So what's on your mind?"

"Actually, two things. One—and this is the most important—it's been too damn long since we've gotten together. How about picking a weekend and coming down here to Indian Creek? We've got some great fishing around these parts and it'll give us a chance to catch up on things."

"Now that sounds like a winner. It'll have to be a couple weeks from now though. I'm teaching a class at the academy the next couple of weekends. I'll be free the end of the month. Would that suit?"

"Terrific. Now, the second reason I called concerns your brother out in California. He's still practicing law out there, isn't he?"

"Ernie. Sure, he's still with the same firm. What do you need a California lawyer for? I didn't think you ever left the United States of Texas."

Kelly laughed. It was an old joke. Kelly wasn't much of a traveler and he'd always claimed that everything he wanted to see he could find in Texas. "I don't need him personally," Kelly said. "What I need is some probate information. I want him to check up on an estate that's just been distributed. Do you think he can get that information for me?"

"Sure. I don't see any problem. Let me grab a pen and paper here. Okay, now shoot."

"The deceased's name was Eleanor Perkins, she lived in San Clemente, California. I don't know the exact date of death but it was sometime last year. The estate has probably been probated within the past two months. What I need to know is what, if anything, Eleanor's brother Frank received out of the estate. Frank Perkins."

"Okay, I'll pass this on to Ernie. Sounds intriguing. Maybe you can fill me in when I get up there."

"It'll be intriguing if Ernie finds out what I think he will. And it just might help solve a murder."

"Are you back on the force?" Jim's voice registered surprise.

"No, not yet. I still haven't made a decision about that. This is something I got involved in because of a friend. You remember Gus, don't you?"

"Sure. How's that old sinner doing anyhow?"

"Oh, he's fine, same as usual. He left the city about three years back. He's a homicide detective with the county now and one of his cases involves a murder at the flea market where

213

I handle security. I've been nosing around a bit—with Gus' blessing, of course—and this Perkins business just might answer a few questions."

"I'll get Ernie on it right away. I'll give him your number so he can call you direct with the information."

"Thanks, Jim. I'll see you the end of the month."

"For sure. You take care now."

Kelly hung up the phone and glanced at his watch. Bubba didn't usually leave the bait house until midnight. He should still be up. "Hey, Jake!" he hollered. "Let's go have a talk with Bubba."

Jake, wide-awake at the promise of a run, raced to the door.

As usual, Bubba sat kicked back in an old wooden chair with his feet propped against the potbellied heater. Kelly stepped in the door and Bubba greeted him with a wide grin.

"Hey, good to see you, Kelly. I was beginning to think I'd have to spend the whole night right by my lonesome. Ain't been a soul around since dinner."

"I figured you might be up to some company." Kelly grabbed a cup off the rack and stepped to the stove. "Is that coffee hot?"

"Yep!" Bubba grinned. "Hot and black like it oughta be."

"I saw Cam earlier tonight." Kelly straddled a chair. "He wasn't any too pleased with the county's hospitality and he sure was glad to get back home."

"Yeah. I talked to him myself. I hope like hell things work out for him."

"I hope so, too. By the way, Cam says Anna had about twenty thousand dollars in that metal box of hers and he doesn't have a clue what happened to that money."

Bubba's face lit up. "Cam told you! Damn! I'm sure glad to hear that, Kelly. I been fretting over that money for days. See, I knew Anna'd put it there but I hated to bring it up what with Cam being in all this trouble. I didn't want to believe he'd stolen it but what the hell else was I supposed to think? Anna'd told me she was putting the money in the box until Monday when that real estate fella was supposed to come and get it, see. Then when she got killed and all that shit came out about Cam taking the note, I didn't know what to think. Nobody said anything about the money and I was afraid to mention it 'cause of Cam."

"You could've told me." Kelly couldn't keep the edge from his voice.

"I thought about it, I really did, but how would that have looked? Cam was counting on you and I figured if you knew about that twenty grand, you might think Cam took it, and then maybe you'd drop the investigation."

"It might have worried me a little but I wouldn't have dumped Cam because of it. Didn't it occur to you that money might have something to do with the murder?"

"Course it did. That's why I kept my mouth shut. I knew Cam must've taken that note, so it kind of figured he took the money at the same time. I could understand all that. He's been having a tough time keeping the bar afloat and we all know what the Hideaway means to Cam. What I wasn't buying, though, was the idea Cam murdered Anna. I know Cam and whatever else he is, he's not a murderer."

"So what do you think happened to the money?" Kelly asked.

"It beats the hell out of me but now I know Cam didn't take it, I sure would like to know who did. The thing is, Anna did say that money was mine. She only put it in the box for safe keeping until Monday when I was going to pick it up. So, if we do find out who took the money, you think there's any chance I might still get it?"

"I don't know, Bubba. I'll have to ask Krystal. She's the beneficiary, so technically, I suppose the money's hers but she's a decent person and if she believes Anna intended the money for you, I think she'd honor her mother's wishes. Of course, first thing we got to find out is who does have that money."

"I know. Like I said, I thought Cam stole it but now I know he didn't, it's a whole different can of worms."

"I do have one idea I'm working on," Kelly said. "But I don't know yet if it's going to lead anywhere."

"What's that?"

"Just something that's been bugging me. That money Frank inherited from his sister. Just out of curiosity, did you ever hear him mention an inheritance from his sister before he suddenly came into the money?"

"Well, I'll be damned! That son of a bitch! I never thought about it before but he never said a word about expecting any money until he bought that fancy boat. I'll kill him myself if he ripped off Anna's money."

"Whoa. Calm down." Kelly put out his hand. "We don't know Frank had anything to do with the missing money. It's just speculation and I think we've had enough killing around this place."

Bubba grinned. "Shucks, I was only letting off steam. I think you might have something, though. What are you planning to do about it?"

"I've already asked a friend on the force to make some inquiries. Like I said, I'm not really sure of anything. It's just suspicion. Now, whatever you do, you keep this to yourself. I don't want you going off half-cocked and jumping Frank before we even know if there's anything wrong with his story."

"Okay. But it's going to be damn hard to do."

Kelly said goodnight and called Jake back from the creek where he'd been nosing around with the ducks and the two of them headed back to the cabin.

Inside, Kelly got a beer and went back to the recliner. Bubba hadn't told him anything new but talking out his suspicious helped him formalize his thoughts. Now, if the beer just helped to make him sleepy, maybe he'd manage to get some shuteye before daylight rolled around.

Chapter Fourteen

Kelly tossed restlessly, chased by dreams. Or maybe he was chasing the dreams. In the depths of shifting light and dark, it was hard to tell. A golden-haired child clutching her stuffed kitty moved into the corner of his vision. She was in trouble. He could see her trembling, hear her rapid breathing. She needed help but she was moving so fast. He had to catch her before she opened that door, the one that just appeared from nowhere. Too late. Her chubby hand pushed against the wood and light from a reading lamp bathed a corner of the room. A man lay on the floor, his head smashed and broken like a Jack-O-Lantern after a fall from the porch on Halloween night.

The child called out. "Daddy!" She bent to pat the man's face, the way little girls always did when waking their daddy up from a nap. Her fingers plunged into a hot, sticky mass, and her hand came away clotted with something slimy. She screamed. The scene shifted and the room morphed into a living thing, a monster, with the mouth of a roaring furnace. It opened its jaws and out of the smoke came Lynda. Her long, blond hair tumbled over her shoulders and fell in golden waves to her breasts.

"Lynda!" Kelly called her name and she floated over the flames and into his arms.

"Oh, my God!" He held her tight. "I thought I'd lost you again."

"You can't lose me," she whispered. "Look!" She pointed toward the fire. Kelly turned and gasped. In the mouth of the beast stood Krystal.

"Kelly!" she called. "Help me, please!"

"No!" The scream tore from Kelly's throat as he fought to free his paralyzed limbs. Then a coarse, wet tongue licked his face and released him from the grip of the dream.

"Damn, that was a bad one," he groaned.

Jake jumped down from Kelly's chair and stood watching while Kelly cleared his head and got to his feet.

"Thanks!" Kelly leaned over and hugged Jake.

He hadn't had one of those dreams in three years and it didn't take a rocket scientist to figure out his relationship with Krystal had been the catalyst.

He almost called her before he looked at the time. Half-past twelve. Nope, too late to call. So what should he do now? Sleep was out of the question. He wouldn't risk having that dream again. And he couldn't shake the feeling he needed to touch base with Krystal.

"I can't help it, Jake," he said. "I feel like an idiot but I'm going to drive on over to the apartment and see if those girls are all right."

He grabbed his jacket and headed outside to get Old Blue. Krystal and Penny would probably be sound asleep but what the hell, the drive would do him good. He needed a chance to calm down and most of all he needed to make sure Krystal was okay.

It was one of those clear, cold nights when the highway rolled like a long, black ribbon under a diamond-studded sky. Kelly cranked his window down and let the cold air blow the gremlins out of his head. He didn't want to think right now. Or even try to. Things were too complicated. He just wanted to feel the cold, hard plastic under his hands and listen to the wind howl through his window.

Even at midnight, traffic zoomed along Jacksboro highway. Most of the bars were still open and the glare of neon lights comforted him. By the time he hit Camp Bowie Boulevard, he'd calmed to the point where he had half a mind to turn around and head back home. But there was still that other half—the part of him that wasn't quite sure about dreams and still recalled the stories he'd heard of otherworldly warnings and strange coincidences. It might be a bunch of crap but Kelly knew he'd never rest until he checked on those girls.

The sirens started about two miles from the apartment. Of course, they didn't mean a thing. Sirens went off all night in the city. Still, they set his nerves on edge and his foot pressed harder on the gas pedal.

The closer he got, the louder the sirens screamed. Kelly couldn't keep the hard knot out of his stomach. Two blocks from the apartment, he gave up all pretense of calm. Fire trucks blocked both ends of the street and screamed into the night.

Kelly slammed on the brakes, rammed Old Blue into a parking space and yanked the door half off its hinges. His feet hit the concrete flying. Across lawns, over retaining walls and past two apartment complexes, Kelly ran like a man with the devil on his heels. When he rounded the corner of Krystal's building, a cloud of thick, black smoke choked the breath out of his lungs. His eyes burned and his breath came in short gasps but he kept running, with only one thought in his head. He had to get to Krystal's bedroom and get her out.

"Please, God," he begged. "Don't let me be too late."

Kelly raced around the complex until he reached the apartment. He stopped outside Krystal's bedroom window, yanked off his jacket, rolled it into a ball and smashed his hand into the glass. He saw the blood spurt up his arm. He felt nothing. Up and over the sill he went, letting go and falling into a pile of downy pillows.

"Krystal!" He screamed her name.

She didn't answer. He crawled off the bed and stumbled across the smoke-filled room.

"Krystal!" He pulled open her closet and groped around inside. "Where are you?" He backed out and started for the door. His hand felt the wall and found the light switch. Choking and retching, he wiped his burning eyes and tried to see through the faint glow of light. Nothing moved. The room was empty. Where was she? Had they gotten her out? He couldn't breathe.

Talking aloud, using his own voice to keep himself calm, he stopped at the door and felt the wood. It burned his fingers.

"No, don't open it," he said, yanking back his hand. "It's too hot. She's not in here. They must've gotten her out. Stop it now. Steady. Don't panic. Got to get back out of here. Back to the window. Okay, careful now, over the sill."

Putting all his strength into the effort, he heaved himself through the window and crashed to the ground.

"Hey!" A fireman grabbed his arms as he struggled to stand. "You can't go in there," the fireman said.

"Penny!" Kelly croaked. "Got to check her room. Where's Krystal?"

"Take it easy," the fireman said, forcing Kelly back to the ground. "Our guys are inside. They'll take care of them. That's a nasty gash on your hand. We better get the medic over here to take a look."

Kelly stared at the blood-crusted wound. The painful throbbing finally registered in his brain but he pushed it aside.

"Look!" he shouted.

Another fireman stood framed in the window of Penny's bedroom with a blanket-wrapped bundle clutched in his arms.

"Medics!" Kelly's companion shouted and raced to help his partner. Seconds later, two white-coated medics rushed up with a stretcher and the fireman handed his bundle out the window. The blanket dropped away and Penny's long black hair fell like a web onto the white-sheeted stretcher.

The medics pushed the stretcher away from the fire and clamped an oxygen mask over

Penny's face. Kelly let out his breath. At least she wasn't dead.

"That's everybody out," Penny's rescuer said to Kelly's companion. "Who's this?" he asked, pointing at Kelly.

"Friend," Kelly choked.

"Okay. Better move back. Your friend is on her way to the hospital."

"Krystal." Kelly managed to control his voice. "Her roommate. Where is she?"

"Sorry. I don't know. She's not inside, though. The apartment's empty. Maybe she's out front."

"Thanks!" Kelly struggled to his feet. "I'll go take a look.

Kelly circled the complex a dozen times while the firemen finished the cleanup. Krystal was nowhere in sight. He approached an onlooker, and borrowed his cell phone to call Gus. He'd blown out of the cabin without his. Gus listened to Kelly's story and asked to speak to the fire chief. Kelly found the chief and handed over the phone. After a short conversation, the chief handed it back to Kelly.

"No one but Penny was hurt in that fire," Gus said. "Krystal must've been out somewhere."

"Are you sure?"

"Positive. The chief says his men have checked all the units. Everyone's safe."

"Thanks," Kelly said, reassured. "I'll head on over to the hospital and check on Penny. Maybe she'll know where I can find Krystal."

"Okay, I'll meet you there. I don't want to get you stirred up again but the chief says they found a gas can in the girls' living room. This could be connected to Anna's murder. I'll want to talk with Penny myself. You're not a relative, so you'll need clearance to get inside. Why don't you wait for me out front?"

"Okay. Thanks, Gus."

* * *

"What happened to your hand?" Gus asked, when he walked up to Kelly in front of John Petersmith Hospital.

"It's nothing," Kelly glanced at the bandage. "Just a cut from breaking the glass in Krystal's window. The medics taped it up."

Gus nodded. "Let's go then. Penny is on the fifth floor."

With Gus in the lead, they strode through the front doors, crossed the crowded lobby and stepped into one of the elevators. On the fifth floor, Gus headed down the hall to the nursing station. A tall, gray-haired nurse looked up from reading one of the charts. Gus pulled out his identification and asked for Penny's room number.

"She's in five-sixteen," the nurse said, satisfied with Gus' credentials. "Straight down the hall and turn to your right. I'll page her doctor."

"Thanks." Gus said and started down the hall with Kelly at his heels.

Gus knocked gently and pushed the door open.

Penny lay on the stark white sheets with her hair fanned out across the pillow. Kelly caught his breath. She looked like one of the china dolls he'd seen in a gift shop.

Gus walked over to the bed and sat down in a chair. Kelly stood back and watched. Penny's arms lay stiff against the sheets.

Gus touched her hand and her eyelids fluttered open. Fear sprang into her eyes and she squeezed them shut. Quickly, Kelly stepped up to the bed and crouched beside her. "It's okay, Penny," he said. "Detective Graham is here with me."

Her eyes opened to narrow slits, then widened in recognition. "Penny, where's Krystal?" Kelly stroked her hair.

"Krissie no home," she said.

"I know." Kelly nodded. "Where is she?"

"Not know. I go shopping. Come home. Krissie say man call from Houston. Talk with her about mother. Krissie go."

"Go where?"

"Not say. Maybe see uncle?"

"She said she was going to see her uncle?"

"No. But she say go to Houston. I think maybe she talk to uncle." Penny's breath had started coming in short gasps.

Gus reached over and touched Kelly's arm. "Better take it easy," he said.

Kelly flushed and drew back. "I'm sorry. I didn't think."

Gus nodded. "I know. Maybe we should wait for the doctor before we ask her any more questions."

Kelly nodded and smiled down at Penny. "Sorry," he said. "I got a bit carried away."

Penny blinked and tried to smile. "I worry for Krissie too. Hurts a little." She placed her hand against her chest.

Kelly stroked her hand and smiled. "Don't talk. I'll find out where Krystal is. She'll go crazy when she hears about you. As far as she's concerned, you're her sister."

Penny smiled a real smile and blinked back tears.

The door to the room swung open and a tall man wearing a white coat strode into the room.

"I'm Dr. Hankins," he said. "You're the police detective?"

"Detective Graham," Gus said, standing and offering his hand. "The nurse seemed to think it was okay for us to wait here in the room."

Dr. Hankins nodded. "She's going to be fine. There was quite a lot of smoke inhalation but we don't expect any permanent damage. We'll keep her a couple of days for observation."

"I'll just ask her a few more questions then," Gus said. "If that's okay?"

"Fine. As long as she stays calm." He stepped up to the bed and bent over Penny. "I've spoken to the university. They've been in touch with your parents and they're flying in from China tomorrow."

"Oh." Penny gasped. "They are frightened?"

"No, they're okay. They just want to be with you. Don't worry now. I'll let you talk to these gentlemen for a couple of minutes, then I want you to get some sleep. Okay?"

"Thank you," Penny said.

"Five minutes." The doctor turned to Gus.

"On the button," Gus said.

Dr. Hankins nodded and strode out of the room.

Gus sat back down in the chair and smiled at Penny. "This man Krystal spoke with on the telephone…did she mention his name?"

"No." Penny shook her head.

"Can you remember what she said about her mother?"

"Say man know why mother killed."

Gus stiffened. "She said that?"

Penny nodded. "I ask her not go but she say she must. I say please call Mr. Kelly but she say no."

Kelly clenched his fists and clamped his lips to keep from interrupting Gus' interrogation.

"What time did Krystal leave the apartment?" Gus asked.

"Maybe ten." Penny squinted, trying to remember. "I make tea after shopping. We sit. Krissie have milk, then say she go. I get very sleepy. Go to bed."

Gus looked at Penny and nodded. "You've been a big help. I don't think we need to bother you any more right now."

Penny looked at Kelly. "You find Krissie."

"You bet I'll find her." Kelly took her hand. "And she'll call you herself, the minute I tell her what happened."

"Thank you." Her eyes fluttered shut.

Kelly and Gus walked quietly out of the room. Outside, Gus turned to Kelly.

"I want to have a word with that doctor before we leave," he said. "How 'bout I meet you down in the lobby?"

"Sure," Kelly said. "I could use some air."

"Okay. I won't be more than ten or fifteen minutes."

Kelly paced back and forth in front of the doors. He almost wished he smoked. Gus' behavior puzzled him. He obviously wanted to ask the doctor something he didn't intend to share with Kelly. Probably something about Krystal. Gus knew Kelly had fallen hard for her. He wouldn't be likely to share any fears he had for her safety. He didn't need to, though. Kelly already suspected that the man who'd called Krystal was the murderer. It scared the hell out of him. And where the hell was Gus? He'd said ten minutes. It had been at least twenty. Damn it all, Gus was a cop. He ought to know Krystal's life could be in danger.

Finally, Gus came through the door and Kelly rushed to meet him. "We need to get going on this," he said. "Krystal's caller is probably Anna's killer."

"Hold on, pal," Gus said. "What do you think I've been doing? I had to ask the doctor some questions. The rest of the time I've been on the phone to Houston. Krystal's uncle hasn't seen her—or so he claims. I didn't like his attitude. The Houston boys are putting out an APB on Krystal. Detective Petrie is getting a search warrant for Andrew's residence and you and I have seats on the three o'clock flight to Houston."

"Why can't we leave right now? There's a flight to Houston every hour."

"I know that but it'll take some time to process the paperwork in Houston. There's no sense us charging in there before that gets done and I've got a couple of things to take care of here before we leave."

Gus reached out and gripped Kelly's arm. "I know it's tough but why don't you go home and crash for a couple of hours? You're a cop, Kelly. Think like one. Krystal's either dead already or she's being held as a pawn in some deeper game we don't know about yet. Either way, you gotta be sharp if you want to help get this killer."

"I'm okay. You're right, though. I'll go get loose for a couple of hours and meet you out at the airport. What terminal?"

"Southwest. We can meet at the check-in counter. Two-thirty'll give us plenty of time."

"I'll be there...and Gus? Thanks."

"Not a problem. See you then."

Chapter Fifteen

Suddenly Kelly had an overwhelming urge to visit Lynda's grave. He didn't stop to analyze why, just jumped in Old Blue and headed out to Floral Hills.

In the months following Lynda's death, he'd spent several hours a week sitting by her grave. He felt close to her there. Kelly knew she wasn't really underneath all that dirt but he liked having a visible point of contact. It gave him comfort.

An old black workman recognized his truck and waved as he pulled onto the grounds. Kelly smiled and waved back. The old man had told him one day that he'd been working at Floral Hills for over thirty years. It made Kelly feel good to know the caretakers here.

When he reached the section that held Lynda's grave, Kelly parked Old Blue and started up the pathway. The trees were shedding their leaves and the grass was dotted with brown and yellow skeletons.

Kelly knelt in front of Lynda's headstone, bowed his head and sent up a prayer. He'd never been sure if anyone heard his prayers but he hoped so. He always felt better after he said one and he supposed that was the main thing.

He sank wearily onto the grass and rested his head against her stone. Floral Hills had a restfulness that seeped into his bones. He could think better here than anywhere else. He needed to do that today. He'd been in turmoil ever since he'd awakened from the dream. What he had to do now was disassociate himself from Krystal and think like a cop.

Penny said Krystal had gone to meet a man who knew something about Anna's murder. Was it the killer? If so, what was the point of the fire? And where did Andrew Davis fit into the picture? Kelly was sure the key to Anna's murder lay in her past. But did it? What about Frank and his mysterious inheritance?

Shaking his head to clear his thoughts, Kelly stood up and brushed himself off. After they found Krystal, he'd take another look at everybody involved in the case. Including his friends at Indian Creek. Right now, all he wanted to do was find her.

He said goodbye to Lynda and headed back to the truck. The trip to the cemetery had helped him clarify his mind and barring evidence to the contrary, he'd decided to believe Krystal was alive. If later events proved him wrong, he'd have to cope but for now he needed a clear head.

With that decided, Kelly's next thought was that Krystal might have tried to call. He hadn't even checked his machine. That galvanized him and he made the trip to Indian Creek in fifteen minutes flat.

In the cabin, the red light flashed on his answering machine and Kelly's heart leapt to his throat. He pushed the playback button and held his breath.

"Kelly," a man's voice came from the tape. "This is Ernie Forbes. Jim asked me to give you a call about that probate matter you were looking into. Everything seems in order as far as I can find out. The estate was probated in April and the property divided between the son and daughter. There was no mention of her brother and there weren't any other beneficiaries. The only other payments were the standard tax and funeral expenses. I hope this helps. Let me know if you want me to do any more digging."

The tape ended and Kelly let out his breath. There weren't any more messages. He had to tell Gus about Frank, but first he had to talk to Bubba. He punched in numbers.

"Hey, Kelly," Bubba said. "I figured you was off somewhere this morning. Jake showed up a couple hours ago and I gave him breakfast."

"Thanks. I've been over at Krystal's. They had a fire there last night."

"No kidding? She okay?"

"I don't know, Bubba. She's missing. Look, I haven't time to explain now but I'm headed for Houston. Keep an eye on Jake while I'm gone, will you?"

"Sure thing. Don't worry, I'll look after things here."

"Thanks, Bubba. I'll be in touch."

Kelly hung up and headed into the bedroom. Thirty minutes later, showered and changed, he climbed into Old Blue, tossed his overnight bag onto the seat and headed for Dallas Fort Worth Airport.

At the airport, Gus waited with news. "Andrew Davis has disappeared," he said after they'd checked in at the Southwest booth and picked up their boarding passes.

"Disappeared? What makes you think that?"

"Two of our Houston detectives went out to his house to pick him up and take him downtown. They figured on having him waiting by the time I arrived. Stella met them at the door and told them Andrew got a telephone call during lunch and right after that, he packed a bag and took off. She doesn't have a clue where he went."

236

"Maybe the telephone call was from Krystal."

"Then why all the secrecy and why the suitcase? There's something else too. The Houston boys asked Stella about how much money Andrew had on hand. She didn't know but she agreed to check with the bank. Turns out that early this morning Andrew withdrew a hundred grand from their savings account."

"Whew! That's a helluva lot of money. Do you think Andrew's paying off a kidnapper?"

"It kind of looks that way. Of course, we haven't any proof there's been a kidnapping but Krystal's disappearance and Andrew pulling that kind of money out of the bank sure raises the possibility."

"So what do we do now?"

"We get that search warrant and do a filter job on the Davis house. The way I see it, there's two ways of looking at this setup. Either Krystal's been kidnapped and Andrew is making the payoff, or Andrew's behind the whole thing and wants to get rid of Krystal."

Kelly flinched and Gus cut himself off. "We'd better get out to the gate," he said. "They'll start boarding in a few minutes."

Chapter Sixteen

They checked into a double at the Holiday Inn. Gus stopped long enough to drop off his bag, then headed downstairs to wait for the official car dispatched to pick him up.

With Gus gone, Kelly picked up the phone and called Stella.

"I'll pick you up in ten minutes."

Kelly locked up the room, left a message with the desk clerk for Gus and stepped out the front door just as Stella's Jaguar swung into the driveway.

"You know what I'd like to do?" she said when he joined her in the front seat.

"What's that?"

"I'd like to take a spin out to the Gulf. There's a quaint little place in Channelview that has the best hot, spiced shrimp you'll ever taste. What do you say?"

"You're the driver." Kelly sighed and leaned back in the seat. His mind could use a break from all the worry and speculation about Krystal and he was sure Gus would appreciate Stella's absence.

"Okay, we're off." Stella laughed and tossed her head like a delighted child.

Mirabelle's was definitely quaint, a gaudy, pink building perched on tall stilts sitting precariously over the water.

"Follow me." Stella lead the way up a set of creaky wooden steps.

"This is some view." Kelly followed her across the partially enclosed walkway onto an open-air patio.

"Kind of reminds you of a garden, doesn't it?"

"That it does." Kelly ran his eyes over the tables. Each one sported a bright yellow umbrella with petals that flapped in the wind like a giant sunflower.

"It's chilly out here." Stella rubbed her arms. "Maybe we should go inside. There's a gigantic fireplace and we can cozy up in front of it and gobble shrimp until we burst."

"Lead on."

Inside, only one other couple was occupied in the food and each other.

"This is living." Kelly sank into one of the cushioned seats and held his hands out to the crackling flames.

Stella ordered a large bowl of shrimp and a couple of cold mugs. With that done, she heaved a sigh and settled back against the cushions. "Have you heard anything from Krystal?" she asked.

"I wondered if anyone had told you."

"Andrew said she was missing. But he didn't seem too worried. I suppose you realize Krystal doesn't exactly feel obligated to keep in touch with her family."

Kelly frowned. "It's too bad you two can't iron out your differences. It'd make life easier for both of you."

Stella shook her head. "Our differences, as you call them, are a little too complicated to iron out. Besides, I'm not the one who's kept the pot boiling, no matter what you've been told about the wicked stepmother and how miserable she made Krystal's childhood. That girl is deeper than you think, Kelly. I wish you hadn't gotten involved with her. She's bad news."

"That's pretty strong stuff." A spark flared in Kelly's eyes.

"Okay!" Stella threw up her hands. "Let's drop the subject. Just remember I tried to warn you. Now, tell me what you're doing in Houston. I'm not dumb enough to believe you came down here just for the pleasure of my company."

"Maybe not exclusively but I had a great time when I was here before and I don't think I've ever danced with a better partner."

"Why, thank you, kind sir," she said, her eyes glistening. "Now how about answering my question?"

"Okay. Time to confess. Gus thinks Andrew might know something about Anna's murder and he's getting a search warrant to go through your house. I'm keeping you out of the way so he can have a free hand."

Stella gaped at him. "You don't pull any punches, do you?" She threw back her head and laughed. "I ought to be mad as hell but what can I say in the face of such honesty? I don't have anything to hide and if Andrew does, that's his problem. At least you've been frank with me. Okay...so the cops are searching the house. What're you doing?"

"Interrogating you."

Stella's eyes flashed. "Oh, you are, are you? Well, in that case, I've got terms."

Kelly smiled. He liked Stella. She had plenty of spunk and he suspected it'd take a lot to throw her off kilter. "I'm listening," he said.

"Okay, I say we head on over to the Longhorn for a couple of hours and do a bit of dancing. Your cop friends won't want me around while they're going through my underwear and since you seem to have been appointed my official babysitter, you might as well keep me occupied."

Kelly laughed. "You've got a deal," he said. "On two conditions."

"What's that?"

"I call Gus and tell him where to find us and you answer enough of my questions to convince me that I'm not entertaining a killer."

"You're on," she said. "Ask away."

"Okay, first question. Where were you the night Anna was murdered?"

Stella smiled. "Let's see. That was Saturday night, right?"

"That's right."

"Well, I guess I could say I was home with Andrew."

Kelly lifted his eyebrow. "Yep, you could, but would it be the truth?"

Her eyes flashed and a smile played at her lips. "No, it wouldn't, but I want your promise if I tell you where I spent the night, it won't go any further than this room."

Kelly shook his head. "I can't do that, Stella. The police are investigating a murder and now Andrew's relationship with Anna has been established, it's important you verify your whereabouts the night she was murdered."

She looked at him for a long minute, then shrugged. "I spent the night with Senator Stegman. I'm sure you can understand why I don't want you passing that along to the cops."

Kelly kept his face expressionless. "Well, since you're obviously not implicated in the murder, I'm sure the police would respect your desire to keep your whereabouts private. I know for a fact Gus would."

Stella laughed and shook her head. "There's no such thing as a confidential statement when it involves a state senator. Your friend Gus might be just as pure as you seem to think he is but he's not working in a vacuum. The minute I put Mark's name down on a piece of paper, somebody's going to see dollar signs and you can bet your sweet ass some lucky reporter's going to buy himself a scoop."

Kelly chewed on his lip. Stella had a point. He'd seen it happen too many times to be naive. Mark Stegman had come in two years ago on a landslide ticket that stood for integrity, decency and family responsibility. A front-page scoop about Mister-Family-Values being shacked up with a married woman would sell a bunch of newsprint.

"I'll tell you what I'll do," he said. "I'll tell Gus and I'll try and get his word that as long as nothing comes up that seriously implicates you in the murder, he'll verify your alibi himself and vouch for your whereabouts without making an official report on the alibi itself. Will that suit you?"

"I guess it'll have to. Now, what's your next question?"

"Actually, you've already answered it. I was going to ask if you could verify Andrew's whereabouts but considering where you spent the night, you can't very well do that, can you?"

"No, I can't. As far as I know, he followed his normal routine. Golf in the afternoon, dinner somewhere with one of his cronies, then home to his office to spend a few hours playing with his toys. He's a computer buff and that's how he spends most Saturday nights, unless of course, we have a dinner engagement...which obviously we didn't."

Kelly grinned. "That's it for the questions. Are you ready to go dancing?"

"I thought you'd never ask," she said and reached for her bag. "Let's go."

"I need to give Gus a call, then we can go."

"Okay. I'll get the car and meet you out front."

"Where are you?" Gus answered on the first ring.

"Out at the channel with Stella. You told me to keep her occupied."

"Yeah, I did but there's been a change in plans. We've found a ransom note. I'd like to have Stella at home in case Andrew tries to get in touch."

"So you were right about the kidnapping?"

"Possibly."

The hesitation in Gus' voice let Kelly know that Gus had reservations.

"What're you going to do now?"

"The note gives us a credible reason to go through Andrew's office. We're heading over there now. Meantime, I'd appreciate it if you and Stella would head over to the house in case Andrew attempts to phone."

"Sure thing. Stella's got her cell, but we'll go back to the house and wait. Will you be on your cell?"

"Yes. I'll get back to you if anything comes up."

"Okay. Good luck."

"Thanks. And don't worry about Krystal. We'll do everything we can."

"I know." Kelly hung up the phone.

"I'm afraid I've got bad news," Kelly said when he climbed into the Jag.

Stella braked and turned to face him. "What bad news?"

"Gus found a ransom note. Krystal's been kidnapped."

"I don't believe it. Why?"

"The usual reason. Money."

"And Andrew's gone to pay the kidnapper?"

"It looks that way."

Stella frowned and shook her head. "That doesn't sound like Andrew. If he got a ransom note, the first thing he'd do would be call the cops and demand they do their duty."

"Maybe the kidnapper convinced Andrew he'd kill Krystal if the money wasn't paid."

Stella kept her eyes fastened on Kelly's for a long moment. "Which would mean Andrew would have control of the business and all the money," she finally said.

"Are you saying Andrew would deliberately allow his niece to be murdered?"

"What do you think?"

"I don't know, Stella. But if you're right, it's more important than ever that you and I get back to the house. Gus is on his way over to Andrew's office to see what he can find there. Meanwhile, he'd like you to stay close to the telephone. If Andrew calls you and he's playing some kind of game with Krystal's kidnapper, maybe you can reason with him."

"He's not in the habit of listening to anything I have to say. But of course, I'll give it a try. I'm not overly fond of Krystal but I don't want anything to happen to her."

"That's my girl." Kelly squeezed her arm. "Now let's get back to the house and hope that Andrew calls."

"Okay, but you drive. I'm feeling kind of shaky right now."

"Sure thing," Kelly said, climbing out of the car and waiting until Stella settled into the passenger seat before sliding behind the wheel.

At the Holiday Inn, Kelly pulled up in front of the lobby and ran upstairs for his bag.

"No messages," he said, back in the car. "Do you need to make any stops?"

She shook her head and they drove the rest of the way in silence.

Chapter Seventeen

"Should I put the car inside?" Kelly asked when he pulled into Stella's driveway.

"Please." She reached into the glove box and pushed the door opener.

Kelly garaged the Jag, got out of the car opened Stella's door and grabbed his bag out of the back seat. "That the way we go?" he pointed at a lighted doorway.

She nodded. "It's open."

Kelly pushed the door open and stood aside for Stella to enter.

She led him into a cozy sitting room furnished with plush leather chairs and a brass fitted bar. "Make yourself comfortable while I check with Maria." She dropped her bag on a table and left the room.

Kelly sank into one of the chairs and clasped his hands behind his head. Thoughts of Krystal and the brief time they'd spent together flooded his mind. He'd been making an effort not to wonder what might be happening to her but here, in the house where she'd grown up, it was impossible to push those thoughts aside.

"No calls." Stella entered the room and walked over to the bar. "What would you like to drink?"

"Coffee. If it's not too much trouble."

"One coffee coming right up." She flashed him a bright smile. "I think I'll have something stronger, though."

Kelly listened to the clink of bottle on glass and the sound of coffee making. After she handed him a steaming mug, he watched her curl up in a chair.

"Well!" She fixed her eyes on his. "Where do we go from here?"

"I want to ask you something and I'm trying to word it so you won't be offended but frankly it's a little difficult considering the subject matter."

Stella tilted her head and gave him a cocky grin. "Why don't you just go ahead and spit it out? That's usually the best way."

Kelly returned her grin. "Okay! What would you say if I suggested Andrew might be setting this whole kidnapping thing up so he can kill Krystal and blame it on a kidnapper?"

"But Andrew was here at home when Krystal was supposedly kidnapped. I can vouch for that myself."

"That doesn't mean he couldn't have an accomplice."

Stella shook her head. "I can't see it. If Andrew was going to commit a murder, he sure as hell wouldn't risk being blackmailed for the rest of his life."

"With everything he has at stake, he might take some risks he wouldn't normally consider. Besides, there are ways he could've arranged the kidnapping without making himself vulnerable. After all, if Anna had told Krystal about her affair with Andrew, there's no telling what Krystal might've done. Could Andrew take the chance they'd talked?"

Stella frowned. "That's true, but why would Anna tell a secret that would probably drive Krystal out of her life for good?"

"I think Anna must have changed a lot over the years she spent at Indian Creek. From what I knew of her, she'd have hated the idea of Krystal trusting Andrew and allowing him to continue running the business. I think she might've been willing to sacrifice her own relationship with Krystal if she thought by speaking out she could get her out of Andrew's clutches."

"You could be right. I didn't know Anna but given the same circumstances, that's probably what I'd have done."

"Okay. Now, what about Krystal? Do you think she'd have kicked Andrew out of the business if Anna had told her the truth?"

"You're damn right she would've. She's got her father so high up on a pedestal she'd probably kill Andrew if she found out he was responsible for Clayton's death." Suddenly Stella stopped. "Kelly, what if Krystal's the one who killed Anna and now she's fixing to kill Andrew?"

"No!" Kelly shook his head. "She's one of the first people Gus eliminated. She was home with her roommate the entire night."

"Maybe the roommate lied?"

"Penny? Not a chance! She's a Chinese girl. An exchange student with a limited command of English. And she's so terrified of the police she'd spill everything she knew in the first ten minutes of an interrogation."

"Didn't you say she was nearly killed in that fire?"

Kelly frowned. "It almost sounds like you want to believe Krystal's guilty."

"That's not fair," Stella snapped. "You asked me what I thought and I've told you the truth."

Kelly nodded. "I know. I'm sorry I growled at you but you and I don't exactly see eye-to-eye with you where Krystal's concerned. Let's just leave it that I've got a cop's instinct for murder and I've spent a lot of time with Krystal."

"She's got some kinks, Kelly. I've told you that."

"Not exactly unexpected, wouldn't you say, given the kind of home life she's had." The remark came out rather like a slap and before Stella could react, Kelly held up his hand. "I'm sorry. That was uncalled for. Let's get back to Andrew, shall we?"

"If you wish," she said, the hurt evident in her voice. "I don't know what else I can tell you. I admit everything you say is possible but that doesn't really get us any closer to this supposed kidnapping of Krystal, does it?"

The telephone rang and Stella turned toward the doorway. "I'll take it in Andrew's office," she said. "Why don't you come along? There's a speakerphone so you can listen in if it's Andrew."

Kelly followed her into the large, well-equipped study. His eyes scanned Andrew's private domain. Along one wall were bookcases, file cabinets and an entertainment center. An antique roll top desk dominated the center of the room and a state-of-the-art computer center covered most of the far wall.

"It's for you." Stella held out the receiver.

"Hello," Kelly said.

"I see you got her there okay." Gus' voice was on the line.

"Sure, no problem. Any news?"

"Nothing much. We went through the offices but didn't find anything out of order. There're a couple of people I want to see as a follow-up but I doubt if they'll lead anywhere. Since nobody's heard from Andrew, the Houston boys are about ready to write the ransom note off as a bad joke on somebody's part."

"They're not serious."

"I'm afraid they are. And that's not all. I spoke with Captain Jeffrey a couple hours ago and he wants me back in Fort Worth tomorrow. There's been a break in another one of my cases and he doesn't have the manpower to cover it without me."

"So where does that leave Krystal?"

"I'm sorry, Kelly but as it stands right now, there's every reason to believe Krystal's absence is voluntary."

"I understand. You won't mind if I stick around for a couple of days and see what turns up, will you?"

"Of course not. That's why I called. My hands are tied but that doesn't stop you. As long as you have Stella's cooperation, you might as well keep after Andrew and see where it leads."

"Thanks, Gus. That's what I was hoping you'd say. Any suggestions?"

"Well, first off, I'd give that house another going over. We went through it rather quickly and maybe missed something. And another thing. Finding that ransom note in Andrew's desk the way we did bothers me. It was too easy. Like someone wanted us to find it. You don't suppose Stella's involved?"

"I doubt it. Not her style. What exactly did it say?"

"If you want to see your niece again, get together $100,000. Instructions will follow."

"Typed?"

"Nope. It was printed in block letters using a thick lead pencil."

"I don't know what to think, Gus. But I'll talk to Stella."

"Good. I'll spend the morning following up the leads we picked up at Andrew's office but if nothing turns up, I'm catch the noon flight back to Fort Worth."

"Good enough."

"Any news?" Stella asked.

"Nothing. They suspect the ransom note might be some kind of a prank."

"A prank? Who'd do something that stupid?"

Kelly blushed and dropped his eyes.

"Wait a minute. Don't tell me those idiots think I might have written that note?"

Kelly grinned and lifted his arm like a shield. "Don't kill the messenger. I didn't suggest anything like that."

"No, but I got the idea from your conversation I was suspected of something."

"Gus thinks there's something fishy about that ransom note, that's all. As it stands, there's been nothing to indicate any real danger to either Krystal or Andrew, except that note and given the backlog of homicides Gus has to deal with, he really can't spend any more time down here waiting for something to happen."

"I suppose you're right." She placed her hand over her mouth to cover a yawn. "I guess I'm too tired to think right now. What do you say we get some sleep? Maybe things will make more sense in the morning."

"That sounds like a winner." Kelly yawned. "You just point me toward a bedroom and I'll be asleep before my head hits the pillow."

Chapter Eighteen

Kelly slept fitfully in the strange bedroom and woke before six. He wandered down the hall and found the kitchen. A pleasant, round-faced woman was wiping down the cabinets and the smell of fresh-brewed coffee tickled his nostrils.

"Good morning! I'm Maria. Would you like coffee?"

"Morning, ma'am. I'd love a cup."

"Ms. Davis generally doesn't come down until after nine but if you'd like some breakfast now, I'll be glad to fix it."

"Coffee's fine." He took the offered mug and smiled his thanks. "I'll just take it to the other room and leave you to your work."

Maria nodded and Kelly headed into the lounge. He felt a little awkward asking Stella to let him search the house. He spent some time trying to figure out how to word his request. Finally, deciding the straightforward approach was always the best one with Stella, he drained his coffee cup and strolled back to the kitchen for a refill.

The room was empty. Maria was apparently working somewhere else. Kelly pulled one of the stools up to the counter and poured another coffee. The telephone buzzed. It sounded like an intercom but Kelly wasn't sure whether he should answer it or not. When it buzzed again, he shrugged and picked it up.

"Is that you, Kelly?" Stella's voice purred in his ear.

"In the flesh."

"Has Maria fixed you some coffee?"

"I'm drinking it right now. Do you want me to bring you a cup?"

"That would be wonderful." Stella sounded pleased. "Take the stairs to the second floor. It's the first door on your right."

"Gotcha! I'll be right there."

Kelly took a cup off the rack, picked up sugar and creamer, placed them on a small tray and got the coffee. Then he carried the loaded tray upstairs and knocked on the door.

The bedroom suited Stella and Kelly could see at a glance that Krystal hadn't exaggerated about Andrew and Stella's sleeping arrangements. There was nothing masculine about this room. A four-poster bed draped in yards of dark yellow satin dominated the room and contrasted nicely with the lemon yellow walls. Stella, makeup applied and hair well brushed, propped herself against a pile of satin pillows.

"Good morning!" She flashed a Pepsodent smile. "This is a real treat."

Kelly bowed and placed the tray on her nightstand. "It's my pleasure," he said and sat down on the bench beside her bed. "How're you feeling this morning?"

"Better now." She reached for the coffee cup. "Did you sleep okay?"

"Like a babe."

"Andrew's assistant needs something out of the safe, so I have to run by there this morning but I'll be back as fast as I can. I suppose you'd better let the answering machine pick up the calls, just in case Andrew tries to get through. When the telephone rings, why don't you go into Andrew's office and listen to the machine? That way, if it happens to be for you, you can intercept the call."

"No problem but I do need to ask you a favor."

"What's that?"

"This is a little difficult but I guess the best way to handle a tough question is to come right out with it."

Stella tilted her head and met his eyes. Her expression was curious but not alarmed.

"Gus figures they might have been a bit too hasty with their search last night and he suggested I might like to have another go at it. That is, if it's okay with you."

For several moments, Stella stared at him over the rim of her coffee cup. Finally, she shrugged. "Suit yourself."

"You don't mind then?"

"Of course I don't mind." Her tone belied her words but after a few minutes of silence she smiled at Kelly and softened her voice. "I shouldn't be more than an hour. You already know where to find Andrew's study and his bedroom is down at the end of this hall. Then there's the attic, if you really want to dig. I don't think Andrew keeps much up there but there's a bunch of junk that belonged to Vivian and of course, what's left of Clayton and Anna's stuff.

"Krystal's bedroom is on the first floor, next to the guest room where you slept last night, if you want to poke around in there."

Kelly nodded. Her voice had sharpened when she mentioned Krystal's room but he didn't react. Krystal was a sore spot between them and he figured the less said about her, the better they'd both feel.

"You're a trooper," Kelly got up from the bench.

"Oh, get out of here and let me get dressed." She tossed her head as if to throw off the compliment.

Kelly grinned and left the room. Downstairs, he headed for Andrew's study. As a cop, he'd searched rooms as a matter of course but he hadn't been a cop for a long time and standing there with his hand on the knob, he struggled with his own discomfort. Finally he shrugged his uneasiness aside and pushed open the door.

He didn't expect to find much considering Gus and the boys had concentrated on this room. He started with the desk. He went through all the drawers, then turned his attention to the files. There were several drawers of them but nothing of interest to Kelly. He continued the search, flipping through all the books on the shelves above the computer center and going through a tall file cabinet. As expected, he found nothing. He'd just finished the last of the files and was trying to figure where to look next when a knock sounded on the office door and Maria peeked her head inside.

"I'm leaving now," she said, "but I've fixed a snack for you and left it on the counter."

"You're a lifesaver." Kelly smiled at her. "I could do with a bite."

"I'll say goodbye then." Maria smiled and pulled the door shut.

Kelly closed up the cabinet. "Waste of time," he muttered as he headed downstairs to find his lunch.

The enticing aroma of fresh bread mingled with the pungent smells of salsa and cilantro filled the kitchen. Kelly sniffed appreciatively and lifted the cloth from a large wooden tray. Thick slices of bread, barbecued ham, jalapenos, olives and a bowl of frijoles topped with grated cheddar were arranged on an oak platter. His stomach growled.

"Now this is what I call a meal." He picked up his fork and tried to convince himself the morning hadn't been a waste.

By the time he finished eating, Kelly'd decided to pass on going through Andrew's bedroom but the attic still intrigued him. Stella'd said Clayton and Anna's belongings were stored up there.

The stairway wound like a snake from basement to attic with steps carpeted so thickly Kelly's boots left an imprint of his passage. On the attic landing, he tried the handle of a plain white door. It swung open and Kelly stepped into a dimly lit, low-ceiling room. Patches of sunlight played across bare wood floors and a brass ceiling fan spun cedar-scented air around the room. He crossed the floor on thick braided rugs that muted his footsteps and stopped in front of a large window seat. A soft pillow covered its wide ledge. Standing there looking at the seat, Kelly could imagine Krystal curled up on the cushion with a favorite book.

He turned his mind back to the business at hand, scanned the room and spotted three garment bags.

"Let's see what we have here," he muttered, opening the first bag. That one held a couple of men's suits.

In the second, he found two formal gowns and a London Fog overcoat. The third bag was more intriguing. It contained an old wedding dress, a bouquet of dried flowers and an antique lace veil. Kelly smiled. Krystal might wear that dress one day.

The far corner of the attic held a stack of trunks and boxes. He moved over and peered down at them. One of them caught his eye because it was tied with a pink rope. He pulled it out and started working on the knots. The strands were tangled but he loosened them enough to slip the rope aside and open the top flaps.

Inside, he found what must have been the contents of Krystal's toy chest. Barbie was there and Ken and Skipper and Barbie's car. A small cardboard closet was filled with Barbie's party clothes. Buried deep in the box was a pink kitten with a long fluffy tail. The kitten's ears were squashed and its fur stuck together. Kelly wondered if late night tears had matted them down like that. He sighed and started to replace kitten and dolls, touched by this glimpse into Krystal's past, even though it was no help with his problem. His fingers tightened around the kitten and some paper rattled. Puzzled, he turned it over. The tail flopped back to reveal a zippered opening.

This was intriguing. Walking over to the window-seat, he sat down and pulled open the zipper. A long white envelope rested inside. Kelly stuck his fingers inside the kitten and tugged. The envelope was in there good and tight but he finally worked it loose. Holding it up to the light, he saw where the flap had been opened and then resealed with strips of tape. He turned it over and squinted at the spidery writing. The barely legible faded ink read "Andrew Davis—Private".

Kelly stared at the envelope. Something was out of kilter here. Why would Krystal hide a letter addressed to Andrew inside her old kitten? A small inner voice suggested he put the envelope back in the box. Kelly shook his head. His other voice, the louder one, told him he'd be a fool to overlook anything that might be a clue to Anna's murder. He folded the envelope and stuck it inside the back pocket of his jeans. Then he packed the toys back in the box, retied the rope and left the attic.

Back in the kitchen, Kelly decided Stella wouldn't mind if he helped himself to a beer. He took one of the cold bottles out of the fridge and contemplated what to do next. He'd found nothing except the letter, which he'd already decided to give to Gus, which would make him feel better about taking it out of Krystal's private box.

"Might as well check the telephone," he muttered and started down the hall to Andrew's office.

He stepped over to the desk and looked down at the flashing light. It hadn't been lit before, so there must have been a call while he was up in the attic. Picking up a pen and getting a piece of paper ready so he could make a note of the calls for Stella, he turned on the tape.

"Stella!" a female voice said. "My car's going to be in the shop tomorrow. Can you pick me up for the luncheon?"

Shaking his head, Kelly pushed the pause button. "A name would have been nice," he muttered. Oh well, Stella probably knew who it was. He jotted down the message and restarted the tape.

"Stella!" The next caller was a man. "It's Andrew," the voice said and Kelly snapped to attention. "Krystal's in trouble. I've gone out to Sea Isle to meet her. You'll have to call the office and tell them I won't be in for a couple of days. I'll give you a call once I've got things straightened out. And Stella…not a word about Krystal. If anybody asks, I'm on a business trip."

The tape stopped but Kelly sat for several minutes staring at the machine. An ugly suspicion had been lodged in the back of his mind ever since last night's conversation with Stella. Now, reluctantly, he let it float to the surface. First Anna's murder, then Penny's narrow escape and now Andrew's mysterious phone call.

What if Stella was right? How well do I really know Krystal? They'd gotten close—maybe too close—in the weeks following Anna's murder. But Stella had known her a lifetime.

Reaching into his pocket, Kelly pulled out the letter he'd taken out of her box in the attic.

Leaving Andrew's office, he started down the hall, something drawing him toward Krystal's bedroom. He'd always had a sixth sense for impending disaster and right now his neck prickled like a spider had crawled down his spine.

Krystal's room was bright and youthful. A border flocked with pink rosebuds circled the walls and frothy pink curtains covered the casement windows. A cream-colored French provincial bookcase stood in the corner, its shelves covered with antique dolls. A writing desk with a small white chair stood in front of the window. Kelly walked over to it and pulled out the chair.

He took a swallow from the beer, set it down and reached in his pocket for the envelope. Inside he found a handwritten letter and a blue bound legal document. Kelly opened the letter. The spidery writing had faded and there were dark splotches on the paper. The writer had used an old-fashioned fountain pen. Kelly squinted his eyes to focus on the words and began to read.

Dear Andrew,

I realize this letter is going to upset you. However, we must all accept our suffering. As you are aware, I'm beginning to suffer some of the deterioration often associated with old age. Therefore, while I still have all of my faculties, I have attended to various legal matters. Undoubtedly, you'll resent my decision.

I am leaving all of my stock in Davis Oil to Krystal. You, of course, will be named her guardian. I have considered this decision carefully. Clayton killed himself because you committed adultery with his wife and I cannot go to my Maker with the knowledge you escaped punishment."

Your Mother,

Vivian Davis

Kelly put the letter aside and picked up the legal document. He read it through quickly and when he came to the signatures, he closed his eyes and dropped it on the counter. In one stroke, Anna Davis had signed away her life, her fortune and her child. The old woman had been thorough and merciless. She'd left nothing to chance. Every detail of Anna and Andrew's affair had been spelled out and acknowledged by both of them.

Tears pricked the corner of Kelly's eyes. He knew the truth now and he had to face it. Krystal hadn't been trying to find her mother to ask why she'd abandoned her. She already knew why. She'd wanted to find Anna to could kill her. Kelly knew it in his gut, just as he knew she'd succeeded. And that she had Andrew.

Chapter Nineteen

Kelly sat in Krystal's room for a long time. In his mind, he recreated all their conversations and the pattern of her lies became clear. All the seemingly innocent remarks she'd made about her Uncle Andrew, the story of her neglected childhood, even their lovemaking, had been designed to enlist Kelly's support and sympathy.

Finally getting a grip, Kelly took the letter and headed downstairs to Andrew's study. He had to get hold of Gus. He walked over to the desk and reached for the phone. He'd call Detective Petrie and see if Gus was still in town

"Detective Petrie is out on a call," the dispatcher told him. "Can I take a message?"

"I'm trying to get in touch with Detective Graham," Kelly said. "Do you know if he's still there?"

"Hold, please. I'll check."

Kelly struggled to get his thoughts in order while he waited. If Gus was gone, what should he do? Kelly's instincts told him Krystal was involved in whatever had happened to Andrew but Detective Petrie wasn't likely to be impressed with his gut feelings. Cops went on facts and Kelly wasn't a cop anymore.

"Hello!" The dispatcher's voice came back on the line just as the door opened and Stella walked into the room. Kelly lifted his hand and motioned her over to the desk. "Did you find him?" he said into the phone.

"Detective Graham left for the airport a couple hours ago," the dispatcher replied. "Would you like me to locate Detective Petrie?"

"No, thanks. I'll try him later." Kelly hung up the phone.

"What's wrong?"

Kelly picked up the letter from where he'd dropped it on the desk and handed it over to Stella. "I found this in Krystal's toy box," he said. "It looks like you were right all along."

Stella read the letter while Kelly sat with his head in his hands trying to figure out what to do next. When she'd finished, she put the letter back on the desk and placed her hand on Kelly's arm.

"I'm sorry."

Kelly lifted his head and looked into Stella's eyes. "Did you know about this?" he asked in a harsh, grating voice he barely recognized as his own.

"No! I didn't know about the letter but I did suspect she'd found out something about Anna and Andrew the last time she was down here."

"Why didn't you tell me?"

"Because you wouldn't have believed me. Andrew's never listened to anything I said about Krystal, so why should you?"

"Andrew's message said something about meeting Krystal at someplace called Sea Isle. Do you know where that is?"

"Andrew's at Sea Isle?"

"That's what he said. Here, I'll rewind the tape and you can listen. Maybe you can figure out where he's planning on meeting Krystal."

"You don't need to." She shook her head. "If he's going out to Sea Isle, he must be meeting her at our beach house. It's called The Last Resort." The name came out as a kind of giggle and she clapped her hand to her mouth. "I'm sorry." She gasped. "I don't know what's wrong with me."

"It's my fault." Kelly went to Stella and put his arm around her shoulder. "I shouldn't have sprung it on you like that. You're shaking all over. Do you want to sit down?"

"No. I'll be all right." Stella leaned against his chest. "Just give me a minute."

Kelly tightened his arms and held her until the shaking stopped. When her breathing slowed to normal, he released her.

"What should we do now?" she asked.

"I think our only choice is to go out to Sea Isle and try to find Andrew," Kelly said. "I could be way off base here but every instinct I have tells me Krystal's up to something. I'll feel like a damn fool if Andrew's off on some romantic rendezvous and I stick my big foot into the middle of your personal life but I can't shake the feeling something stinks to high heaven.

"Oh, don't worry about that. I'm so used to Andrew's antics it wouldn't faze me even if I caught one of his bimbos sneaking down the back stairs." Stella's spirits rose at the thought of Andrew pulling one of his tricks and she actually grinned at Kelly. "Do you want me to call the beach house?"

"No. I don't think that's a good idea. When Andrew called, he said he was on his way to Sea Isle to meet Krystal. If he's out there to meet someone he's not likely to admit it to you. Maybe the whole thing about Krystal is a blind. I'd just feel better if we checked it out. That's all. Is there any way to get up to the house without Andrew—or Krystal for that matter, if this is an innocent misunderstanding—knowing we're there?"

"Sure. The beach area's wide open but the Shelton place is next door. They're good friends of ours and I've got a key to their house. If Andrew's down there, we'll see his car from the main road and we'll have a clear view of the place from the Shelton's front room. Maybe we'll spot Andrew and either Krystal or his latest companion."

"I'm sorry, Stella."

"Hey, don't be. I'm used to it. Besides, as you've probably figured out, I'm no saint myself. I will tell you one thing though. If Andrew's up to something, I'll bet it involves somebody else's wife."

"Why do you say that?"

"Because he sure as hell wouldn't go to all this trouble just to pull the wool over my eyes. Things are way past that stage in our household."

"Another question. I don't want to spook you, but we are dealing with a potential kidnapper. Since I flew up here I didn't bring my gun. You don't happen to have one here in the house do you?"

Stella's eyes widened. "You're not going to shoot him."

"I'm not planning on shooting anyone. But we don't know what we'll find. Do you have a gun?"

"There's one locked in the desk." Stella took a key from Andrew's desk and unlocked one of the drawers in his file cabinet.

"I don't like guns, but Andrew insisted on having one." Stella pulled a revolver out of the drawer and handed it over to Kelly.

"I'm sorry to drag you into this," he said, "but I'll feel better once we make sure everything's okay out there."

"I don't mind," Stella said. "I think you're wrong, but what if you're right? Andrew's a bastard but if Krystal is out to kill him, the least I can do is warn him."

Taking I-45 South from Houston, they crossed the Galveston Causeway, took 61st Street to the beach and followed the seawall until it turned into FM 3005.

"It's about five miles ahead on the beach," Stella said.

As they drove, Kelly thought back to the time he'd spent with Krystal, trying to reconcile what he thought he knew about her to what he'd just found out."

"It's tough, isn't it?" Stella seemed to read his thoughts.

"I guess I'm having a hard time realizing I could've read someone as wrong as I did Krystal. Do you really think she's capable of murder?"

"Yes!" The word came out hard and brittle. "I'm sorry, Kelly. But there's a side to Krystal most people never see. When she was small, she'd do mean, spiteful things, like breaking ornaments in my room and stealing my jewelry and throwing it into the trash. But as she got

273

older, her pranks got more vicious. I used to have a toy poodle I adored and one night she disappeared. I was frantic. I searched for Mitzi for weeks but I never found a trace of her. That spring the landscapers called me out to the back yard. They'd been digging in one of the flowerbeds and found Mitzi's remains. I suspected Krystal immediately. She knew how much I loved that dog. But of course I couldn't prove anything."

"Didn't you at least discuss it with Andrew?"

"What for? He'd never have believed me. Remember, Krystal's the heiress. Andrew always took her side against mine. Besides, what was the point? Mitzi was dead. Nothing I did was going to change that. Things were difficult enough right then. Vivian'd already started going downhill and she absolutely refused to let the nurses take care of her personal needs, so most of it fell to me."

"I thought she hated you?"

"She did, but I guess over time she'd gotten used to having me around. Toward the end, it got so bad I was the only one who could touch her."

"That must've been tough on you."

"It was. Anyway, to get back to Krystal. One night after I'd finished settling Vivian in for the night, I went to my room to get dressed. Andrew and I had a dinner engagement and when I went to put on the dress I planned to wear, I found a big tear under the arm. Krystal was always getting into my closet and taking my clothes without asking and that night, I exploded. Vivian'd been difficult all day and I simply couldn't take anymore. I went in Krystal's room with the dress under my arm and started screaming at her. She just sat there on the bed and smirked."

Stella hesitated, obviously embarrassed at her own confession and Kelly patted her shoulder. "Go ahead," he said. "I'm not making judgments."

"I don't know what got into me but something seemed to snap and I lost control. I dropped the dress and leapt onto the bed and the next thing I knew we were pulling hair and screaming."

Without thinking, Kelly chuckled and Stella flashed him an angry glare.

"Sorry!"

"I suppose it does sound funny but believe me, at the time it wasn't. Krystal's younger and stronger than I am and within a few minutes she had me flat on my back with her legs straddling my chest and her hands wrapped around my throat. It was like she'd gone insane. She kept squeezing as hard as she could and just before I blacked out, she put her face right down next to mine and said 'Now you can go be with your precious Mitzi.'"

"You must've been terrified."

"I was too busy trying to breathe to realize how scared I was. I found out later the only reason she didn't finish me off was because Andrew heard all the commotion and came into the bedroom and stopped her."

"Wasn't that enough to convince Andrew she had a problem?"

"Of course not. Krystal showed him the dress I'd dropped on the floor and told him I'd attacked her for wearing my dress. I ended up getting a lecture about controlling my temper. There wasn't any point in arguing about it. What could I prove and what would it accomplish anyhow? I knew for sure after that episode that there was something seriously wrong with Krystal."

"You poor kid," Kelly said. "I could kick myself for not listening to you earlier but I was too caught up in my own fantasy. I'm not very proud of myself right now."

"You're not to blame. Krystal's very good at winning people over when she wants to, so how could you, a relative stranger, be expected to see her dark side. Andrew's the one who's blind. He's lived with Krystal for years and if he wasn't such a self-centered, pompous jerk, he'd have realized a long time ago she had some serious problems."

Suddenly, as if realizing what she was saying, Stella gasped. "I can't believe I said that. For all we know Andrew's life is in danger and here I am calling him a jerk. I'm scared, Kelly. Talking about Krystal's made me remember what she's capable of. I think maybe we should call the police."

Kelly shook his head. "And tell them what? She has an alibi for the night of Anna's murder and even though I'm positive she somehow managed to trick Penny into lying for her, I don't have any proof."

"What about the letters you found in her toy box?"

"They won't mean a thing to the police. They might even suspect you put them there yourself."

Stella clutched his arm. "You don't believe that do you, Kelly?"

"No, I don't." He shook his head. "I've had time to realize how easily Krystal manipulated me into believing what she wanted me to believe. But knowing what she's done and convincing the police are two different things. Right now, what we need to do is find out what's really going on with Andrew."

"There it is," Stella said, pointing to a blue-and-white beach house perched on tall stilts at the edge of the water. The two-story building, with its peaked roof and wraparound balcony, resembled a modern schooner.

"Nice," Kelly said.

Stella nodded. "We don't use it much but I love it out here, especially late in the fall when the tourists are gone."

"There's a car parked around the far side. Can you tell if it's Andrew's?"

"I'm not sure. It looks like it but we need to get closer."

"Is that the Shelton place?" he pointed to a bungalow off to their right on the high side of the beach.

"Yes. That's the one. There's a driveway about a hundred yards ahead. It's not marked, so be ready to turn when I yell."

Kelly slowed the car and kept his eyes peeled for signs of a track.

"Stop, turn here!" Stella let out a yelp.

Kelly swerved to the right and eased the Jag onto a narrow ridge of hardened sand.

"Pull around to the far side. That way we'll be hidden from the beach house."

Kelly nodded, followed the track around the house and pulled up next to a small shed.

"I think the house is empty but I'll go knock just to be sure." Stella got out of the car and headed toward a set of wooden steps that led to the back door.

Kelly watched as she climbed the steps and rapped loudly on the door. She waited a few minutes, then took out her key, opened the door and called out. Satisfied, she waved her arm as a signal for Kelly to join her.

"Come through here." She motioned him through the small, narrow kitchen into a large wide-open room with a panoramic view of the beach.

"That's just what we need." Kelly nodded approval when Stella stopped in front of a large telescope.

"We won't be able to see inside the bungalow because we keep the windows shuttered on this side but once I get into position, I'll be able to tell if that's Andrew's car," Stella said.

"Good! There doesn't seem to be any activity around there and only one car. Hopefully, that means Krystal hasn't arrived yet."

"It's Andrew's, all right," Stella said. "I really think, under the circumstances, it would be better if I went over there alone."

"I guess that's a good idea but I'm coming with you anyway. At least as far as the back door."

"Okay, he won't be watching the back anyhow if he's waiting for Krystal. I'll try to talk to him but don't expect too much. Even after I explain, he's not likely to believe me and he's going to be really mad."

"That's fine. At least he'll be warned. If nothing else, he'll probably tell Krystal. Knowing what we suspect might stop her from killing Andrew."

"Let's go then. If I put it off any longer, I'll get cold feet."

Chapter Twenty

"We'll go down the beach and come up behind the house. That's the best way to keep from being seen," Stella said.

Kelly followed her along the patio and off the back steps to a hard packed path that led from the bungalow down to the beach.

"At least it's deserted." They left the path and made their way toward the beach house.

"This is a fairly private area," Stella said. "During the summer season we get a few visitors but not many. Too far off the beaten path for most of the tourists."

"I don't see any sign of life."

"Which could mean Andrew's busy inside," Stella said. Kelly noted the edge to her voice.

"You want me to go inside and scout around?"

"No. I'll go. If he's in there with someone, I'll make enough noise to give him time to hide the bimbo and get decent."

Kelly reached out and squeezed her shoulder. "I'll be right outside the door. If you need me, just yell."

"I will. Don't worry." They reached a plain white door and Stella inserted her key in the lock, turned the knob and stepped inside.

Kelly leaned against the wall and flexed his arms. The tension had his muscles so tight he yearned for a punching bag. Minutes passed and Kelly kept pacing. Finally, after what seemed like hours, he returned to the door and opened it wide enough to stick his head inside.

Damn. What the hell was taking so long?

A long piercing scream echoed through the house and Kelly catapulted into action. Yanking the revolver out of his jeans, he barreled through the door and lodged his back against the wall while he surveyed the scene. A large freezer and a couple of gleaming stainless ovens told Kelly he was in some kind of kitchen. After a quick scan of the room, he made for an archway that led into the main living area.

Kelly stuck his head around the door frame and made a quick scan of the room. He saw no one and crept across to a winding staircase leading to the upper floor. He mounted the steps and moved carefully upwards until he reached the second floor, where he paused and motionlessly listened. A low moan sounded in the distance and Kelly moved toward the sound. Halfway down the hall, he spotted an open doorway.

The scene inside spoke for itself. A man lay sprawled across the bed and Stella sat beside him, holding his lifeless hand. Kelly put the revolver back in his pocket and crossed to the bed.

"He's been shot," Stella managed.

Kelly stood beside her and peered down at the slim, gray-haired man on the bed. A dark stain covered the front of his shirt and his eyes stared blankly at the ceiling. In his left hand, he held a chrome-plated revolver.

"Was Andrew left-handed?" Kelly asked.

Stella nodded. "You don't think he shot himself, do you?"

"No," Kelly said. "But somebody wants us to think he did."

"Krystal?"

"That's my guess but we'll leave it to the police. I'll have to call them soon."

"I know. I'm sorry about the screams. It was just such a shock."

"Of course. No matter what your problems, you weren't prepared for this."

Stella sniffled and nodded. "There's a phone in there." She pointed to a door across the room.

The room was a small office. At the desk, Kelly picked up the telephone and pressed the button marked Police. He reported in to the dispatcher and gave the beach house address. Then he called Gus.

"Where the hell have you been?" Gus snapped.

"Just listen a minute and I'll tell you," Kelly said.

"No. You listen. I've been calling the Davis house for an hour. There's no easy way to tell you this and besides, you're a cop, so you ought to be able to take it. Before we went to Houston, I asked Penny's doctor to run some tests. The results confirmed my suspicion that Penny was drugged the night of the fire and that's not all. I had another chat with Penny. I had to drag it out of her but she finally admitted to leaving the apartment for several hours the night of Anna's murder. I guess you realize what that does to Krystal's alibi. I have to tell you Kelly, I've had doubts about her story all along and frankly, I'm a little worried about your involvement."

"Don't be. I think she killed Anna."

"You what?"

"That's why I'm calling. I took your advice and made another search of the house and I found some letters hidden away in Krystal's things up in the attic. She knew all about Anna's affair with Andrew, don't know for how long, but she knew. While I was up there Andrew called and left a message on the answering

284

machine to tell Stella he was meeting Krystal out at their beach house in Galveston."

"So how does that add up to Krystal killing Anna?"

"Because Krystal wasn't looking for Anna to find out what happened the night her father committed suicide. She already knew. So hire a detective to find her mother? I went back over everything she's told me since the night of the murder and the only thing that makes any sense at all is she's been manipulating all of us into helping her get revenge on both her mother and her Uncle Andrew."

"And how do you figure she expected to pull that off?"

"By killing Anna in such a way that Andrew would be arrested for her murder."

"But that hasn't happened. We've been checking him out but at this point he's only one of several suspects including, I might add, Krystal herself."

"I know, which is probably why Krystal's been so willing to help me in my efforts to clear Cam. She's the one who pointed me toward Andrew in the first place. I'd never have tumbled to his affair with Anna if Krystal hadn't set me up with Stella."

"What about the fire in the apartment?"

"To get rid of Penny. Krystal knows Penny is terrified of the police and once it became apparent you hadn't settled on Andrew as the killer, she realized how much danger she'd be in if you decided to put Penny through another grilling."

"That checks. Penny tried to hold out but when I put the screws to her, she admitted she'd left the apartment right after Krystal went to bed. Penny spent the biggest part of the night watching movies with a neighbor. Krystal could have left the apartment and driven out to Indian Creek to kill Anna real easy without Penny knowing anything."

"Exactly! I think Krystal told Penny she was going to take a sleeping pill, knowing Penny wouldn't bother her for anything less than an earthquake. The rest was easy. It's only a twenty-minute drive from the apartment to Indian Creek and we only have hearsay to tell us Anna was going to the flea market to get her cash box that night. Could just as easy been a meeting with Krystal. We all noticed how strange Anna was acting Saturday night. A call from Krystal would sure explain that. Anyway, no matter how it was arranged, Krystal met her mother, strangled her and in less than two hours, was back home in bed."

"Not bad," Gus said. "It could've happened exactly like you say. So what about Andrew and the kidnapping?"

"I think Krystal got tired of waiting for you to charge Andrew with the murder and decided to arrange an elaborate suicide. That's why Stella and I came out to the beach house. To find Andrew and try to warn him."

"Did you find him?"

"Yes."

"Good. Keep him there. If your surmises are right, that girl's a loose cannon. He could be in real danger."

"It's too late for that Gus. He's dead."

"Murdered?"

"I think so. It's supposed to look like suicide but my guess is murder."

"Have you called it in?"

"Yes. The local police are on their way."

"Okay. Stay there. I'll get hold of Petrie. Any sign of Krystal?"

"No. Gus, is Penny still in the hospital?"

"No. She's staying in a dorm at TCU. Why?"

"I don't know. Call it a gut feeling but it might be a good idea to make sure Penny's somewhere safe."

"Good thinking. I'll get right on it. What's the phone number where you are?"

Kelly read off the number and promised to give Gus a call before heading back to Houston.

The first police car arrived fifteen minutes later and for the next two hours, they answered questions and waited. The county coroner came and took Andrew's body. Finally, when all the official cars had departed, Kelly and Stella were left alone in the beach house.

"I can't even think anymore," Stella said. "I'm completely drained."

"I know. As soon as you're ready, we'll get out of here." The telephone rang and Kelly looked at Stella. "Do you want me to answer?" he asked.

She nodded.

"Davis residence," Kelly said.

"Kelly, this is Gus. I've got bad news."

"What?"

"Krystal's got Penny."

"Got her! What do you mean?"

"Krystal arrived at the dorm a couple of hours after I'd spoken with Penny. It was before we could warn her. The housemother doesn't have any idea where they went. All Penny told her was that her roommate was taking her out for dinner and she'd be back later this evening.

"I've put out an APB on both girls but it doesn't look good, Kelly. We've no idea where Krystal might have taken Penny and if she's left the rails completely, there's no telling what she might do."

"I know. Look Gus, I'll be home on the first plane."

"Okay. Give me a call as soon as you get in. I'll leave instructions to put you through no matter what I'm doing."

Kelly hung up and turned to Stella.

"What's wrong?" Her voice sounded scared and all the color had drained from her face.

"Krystal picked up Penny from the dorm at Texas Christian before Gus could get back to her and nobody knows where they've gone."

"Oh, no! She means to kill her, too, you think?"

Kelly nodded. "That's exactly what I think. Krystal got Penny to swear they were together the night Anna was murdered but she knows if Gus gets hold of Penny and starts putting the screws to her, she'll fall apart."

"But I thought Gus already knew that Penny lied?"

"Sure. But Krystal doesn't know that. Krystal's smart enough to realize if Penny's dead, a good lawyer would make a mockery of Gus' claim that she had recanted her statement."

"So what're you going to do?"

"Get back to Fort Worth as fast as I can. If you're ready, I'd appreciate it if you'd drop me off at the airport."

"I've got a better idea. Why don't you let me drive you?"

"Thanks. But I need to get there in a hurry."

"That's just it," Stella said. "By the time you fool around getting to the airport, getting a seat on the plane, waiting for it to take off, then getting into DFW and finally getting to Fort Worth, we could drive the Jag there and beat that time by an hour or more. Besides, I know Krystal better than either you or Gus. Maybe I can help."

Kelly started to shake his head then he stopped and frowned. "Maybe you're right," he said. "Come on then, let's get started."

Chapter Twenty-One

"Somebody up there must be on our side," Kelly muttered as Stella squealed off the I-20 exit and onto the loop headed for Fort Worth.

"I saw you holding onto the seat back there," she said, a momentary grin flashing across her face. "Thank heavens, all the traffic cops seem to be on holiday. Where to now?"

"We'll take 28th Street up to the White Bull. It's open till midnight and I'm sure you could use a coffee and a bite to eat. I'll give Gus a call from there."

"That's fine. Just tell me where to get off this loop."

Fifteen minutes later they pulled up in front of the White Bull and Kelly led the way to his and Gus' favorite booth.

"I'll take the special," Kelly said. "Why don't you go ahead and order while I call Gus?"

Stella nodded and picked up the menu. When Kelly returned, he shook his head and slid into the booth. "No news. They've completely disappeared. I sure hope they haven't headed for Houston."

"Do you think that's likely?"

Kelly shrugged. "I don't know what to think. What about you? You got any idea what Krystal might do in these circumstances?"

Stella frowned. "It's funny how you can think you know someone and yet when it comes to something bizarre like this, you realize you don't really know them at all. Still, Krystal might try to convince Penny Anna's killer's after her and she needs Penny's help to save her own life."

"Which means she probably won't kill Penny until she can set it up so it looks like Penny was killed by the kidnapper."

"I don't understand. I thought Krystal invented the kidnapping in order to get Andrew out to the beach house."

"That's true, but she doesn't know we know that. As far as Krystal's concerned, the police are still searching for the kidnapper. Now that Andrew's dead, the only way she can make the kidnapping story work is to produce a kidnapper."

"How can she possibly manage that?"

"There's only one way. By choosing someone who fits the profile of the kidnapper, then killing him."

Stella gasped. "You make her sound like some kind of a monster."

"She is. She's a murderer. And that makes her a monster. Not only that but judging from the way she's been manipulating everybody, she's an incredibly smart murderer."

"Krystal's always been clever. If she makes up a story, you better believe it'll be a good one."

"I just wish I could think of where she might take Penny." Kelly picked up his fork. The waitress sat their food on the table. Automatically, without even noticing what was on the plate, he began to eat.

Stella picked at her own food. For several minutes they ate in silence, each absorbed in private thoughts. Finally, Kelly put down his fork and slid out of the booth. "I'm going to call Bubba. Maybe somebody out at Indian Creek has seen her."

"Do you think she'd go there?"

Kelly shrugged. "I don't know. But I can't think what else to do. Gus has got the city covered. If nothing else, at least I can find out how Jake's been holding out."

When he returned, he picked up the bill and helped Stella on with her coat.

"Where to now?" she asked.

"Indian Creek. Bubba didn't answer. And that's strange by itself but he might be up at the Hideaway. We'll stop there and then I guess we wait. Maybe by the time we get to the cabin Gus will have some news."

Stella followed him out to the car and handed over the keys. "You drive. It'll be easier since you know where you're going."

Kelly nodded took the keys and opened the door to let Stella into the car. Kelly drove in silence, lost in thought.

"I'll just be a minute," he said, when they pulled up in front of the Hideaway. "I don't imagine you feel like meeting any strangers."

"No, thanks." Stella settled back in the seat. "I'll just wait out here."

Five minutes later, Kelly climbed back in the car. "Bubba hasn't been around. We'll go to the cabin and I'll give him a call."

When Kelly turned into the drive leading to the flea market, he drove straight up the hill to the cabin. "I'll park the car right here in front just in case we have to leave in a hurry." He reached for the door handle.

The minute he opened the car door, the frantic barking and yapping of a dog going nuts assaulted their ears.

"What the hell?" Kelly jumped out of the car and raced for the cabin. "You stay there," he yelled over his shoulder at Stella as he bounded up the steps.

Grabbing the knob, he yanked open the door and Jake leapt through the opening, nearly knocking him off the porch.

"Hey!" Kelly shouted but Jake kept on going, racing at top speed across the stretch of grass that fronted the cabin and clear on down the hill.

He watched until Jake stopped in front of the main entrance to the flea market, then turned and ran back to the car.

"I want you to go inside the cabin and call Gus."

"What's wrong?" Stella's voice shook and she wore the scared expression of someone waiting for an explosion.

"I think Krystal's inside the flea market. Gus' number is in the book beside the phone. Call him and tell him I've gone in after her. Then you stay in the cabin until I get back." Without waiting for an answer, Kelly turned and started down the hill after Jake.

Jake stood guard beside the front door at the main entrance. He growled low in his throat when Kelly reached him and lifted his front paw to scratch at the door.

"Take it easy, boy." Kelly grabbed the wooden handle and gave the door a yank.

The padlock Kelly'd left securely fastened the day before was unlocked and hanging in the clasp. The lock hadn't been forced, so whoever was inside had used a key. Or been forced to use a key. If it was Bubba, as Kelly suspected, he wasn't alone or Jake wouldn't be raising such a racket.

"Wait here." Jake whined, but sat and Kelly stepped inside and pulled the door shut behind him.

The barn was pitch dark. Kelly groped for the flashlight he kept on a shelf by the door. When he had it in hand, he clicked on the beam and focused it across the barn. Pale yellow light spilled across rows of sheet-covered tables turning them into ghostly shadows. Kelly stopped and took off his cowboy boots. He carried them with him as he made his way noiselessly across the concrete until he reached the shops on the far side of the building. A sound like the thump of someone bumping into a table split the silence and echoed through the barn. Kelly stooped and put his feet back in his boots. Then he listened. He made his way to the light post beside the refreshment stand and decided it would be better if she knew someone was here. He flicked the switch. Nothing happened.

"Krystal?" His voice rang loud in the silent barn. If Bubba and Penny were still alive, Krystal wouldn't kill them if she knew he was in the building. He hoped.

Kelly called her name again and waited. She didn't answer and he started forward again, moving slowly in the direction of Anna's stall. At the refreshment stand, he stopped and peered through the serving window. The old refrigerator cast its shadow across the tiled floor and his light glinted on the stacks of pots and pans lining the shelves.

Kelly listened for a minute, then moved around to the small outdoor patio where Luis Morales served up the best hot tamales in Texas. His stomach muscles clenched from anxiety. Kelly focused his eyes on the row of shops running along the wall next to the refreshment stand. One glance was all it took to confirm his hunch. Light came from under the curtain that covered the front of Anna's shop.

He reached into his pocket and took out his revolver. He crossed the aisle and stopped in front of the shop. Parting the curtain, he peered into the room. No sign of Krystal but Bubba was on the floor, curled up in a fetal position with blood seeping from the wound on his head. Kelly tightened his grip on the revolver and resisted the urge to rush to Bubba's side. He kept his eye on the private enclave at the back of the room where Anna used to do her paperwork and Kelly sidled into the room. He crouched with his back against the wall.

With the full room in view, Kelly saw Penny sprawled in Anna's rocker, a blanket thrown over her shoulders and her head slumped against her chest.

Kelly listened for several moments but there was still no sign of Krystal. Finally, unable to stand it any longer, he crept across the room, grasped Bubba's hand and wrapped his fingers around his wrist. Thank God. Bubba's pulse was faint and rapid and that wasn't good, but at least he was still alive.

He took off his jacket and covered Bubba as best he could, then crossed to Penny. When he bent his head and placed his ear against her chest, he heard the reassuring thump of her heartbeat. She'd been drugged from the looks of it but she was alive.

"Stand right there!" Krystal's voice, cold as ice, came from behind him. Kelly moved his arm. "Keep your hands where I can see them!"

He stopped and stood motionless.

"Now turn around. Slowly."

Kelly turned and faced the girl he'd thought he loved. Now he was looking at a stranger. Her wide green eyes stared unblinking into his and her face flushed with a feverish glow.

"Put the gun down on the floor." She pointed a small pistol at Kelly's head. He hesitated and she stiffened her arm. "I'm an expert shot. Don't force me, Kelly."

Kelly crouched and laid his gun on the floor.

"Back up." Krystal moved forward and shoved the gun away with her foot.

Kelly backed against the wall. He didn't take his eyes off her.

Bubba groaned and Kelly turned his head to look at his friend. "At least let me see to Bubba."

"Why? He's not going anywhere." She waved the gun in a manner that made her meaning clear.

"Gus is on his way."

She tossed her head. "Then I'll just have to work faster." She waved the gun again. "Get over there beside Penny and squat on the floor with your back toward me."

Kelly complied.

"Now give me your hands."

Kelly extended his hands behind his back. She moved up behind him and his muscles tensed as he felt the smooth fiber of a nylon cord being wrapped around his wrists.

"Now back up against that chair and bend your head."

Kelly did as she ordered.

Krystal tugged the rope, taking up the slack until the fibers cut into Kelly's flesh. "There!"

She moved back in front of him. "That rope's wrapped around Penny's neck, so if you've got any ideas about trying to break loose, you better be prepared to strangle her."

Bubba moaned in the background and Krystal strode over to him. She stood for a minute, then bent down and picked up a flat piece of board. "We can't have you waking up right now," she said in a high, taunting voice. Then she lifted the board high in the air and brought it down on the side of Bubba's head.

Kelly jerked forward, felt the rope tighten and forced himself back against the chair.

"What was the point of that?"

Krystal ignored him and Krystal walked over to Anna's cubbyhole and disappeared behind the wall. When she came back in his view, she carried a large gas can.

"What are you doing?" Kelly asked.

She stopped and stared. Her wild, dilated eyes looked right through him. "Why couldn't you have stayed out of this?"

Kelly shuddered. Her intent was clear. She was going to set fire to the flea market and if Gus didn't get here soon, he and Bubba and Penny would all be dead. Kelly's only hope was to keep her talking.

"Why did you bring Bubba into this?"

"That nasty man." She spit the words out. "He's the kidnapper and he's going to die in the fire. I'll tell the police Penny and I came here looking for you and he trapped us inside this barn. Of course I'll get away, and I'll be so sorry I wasn't able to save Penny."

"That won't work, you know," Kelly said.

"Why not? Because you're here? Why did you have to come? By morning, it would've been all over and things could've still been good between us. Now I'm going to have to tell the police you came in here trying to save me and that man jumped you and got your gun away. Then he shot you."

Kelly shook his head. "Gus already knows the truth, Krystal. I found the letters you'd hidden in your toy box. After I read them, I knew you'd killed your mother. Gus has them now, so there's nothing for you to do now but give yourself up. It's too late for Anna and Andrew but Penny and Bubba don't have to die. They've never done you any harm and Penny's been your friend. You don't want to kill her, Krystal. You know you don't."

"How would you know what I want? You're just like all the rest of them. Always telling me what's best for me. Penny wasn't my friend. She told on me! A friend wouldn't do that. Now shut up. I don't want you to talk anymore!" Krystal's

301

voice had risen to a shriek. The look on her face sent Kelly into silence.

He'd done his best. All he could do now was pray Stella had gotten hold of Gus. At least Krystal didn't know Stella was up in the cabin. Maybe, if they were lucky, she'd see the flames and get help before it was too late.

Chapter Twenty-Two

Inside the cabin, Stella glanced around the small living room and spotted the telephone on a table next to Kelly's rocker. An address book lay beside the phone. She picked it up and flipped the pages until she found Augustus Graham and put her finger on the spot.

She leaned against the arm of the rocker while she counted the rings.

"Hello!" A warm, womanly voice answered.

"May I speak to Detective Graham?" Stella asked.

"He's not here right now. Would you like to leave a message?"

"Oh!" Stella wasn't sure what she should do. "Do you have any way of reaching him?"

The woman hesitated. "Is this something to do with his job?"

"I'm sorry," Stella said. "I should've identified myself. My name is Stella Davis and I'm calling for Kelly McWinter. We're out at Indian Creek. He asked me to call Gus and tell him to get over here right away."

"Oh, dear!" The woman's voice held genuine concern. "Gus took one of the little boys from Big Brothers out to a ball game. He has his phone with him though. I'll give him a call. Is Kelly okay?"

"I don't know. Can you please tell Gus Kelly's located Krystal inside the flea market and gone in after her."

"Of course. I'll get Gus. Relax and don't worry. Kelly has a cop's instincts, he won't put himself in harm's way without a backup."

Stella said goodbye and hung up. She spotted an old jacket hanging on a hook, slipped it over her shoulders and let herself out of the cabin.

The path was only dimly lit by moonlight. She stepped carefully to keep her footing and made her way down the hill. Jake stood guard at the entrance to the flea market and Stella bent to introduce herself. Jake sniffed her hand and after satisfying himself with their acquaintance, he bent his head to accept an ear rub.

"What do you think, Jake?" Stella asked. "Should we go inside and see what Kelly's up to, or should we stay out here and wait?"

In answer, Jake stepped over to the door and turned to Stella with an expectant look in his eye.

"I guess that means yes, huh?" She grabbed the wooden handle and tugged open the door. She stepped into the darkness and saw nothing but shadowy images of the long rows of tables.

"Wait a minute," she whispered to Jake. She pulled her key ring out of her shoulder bag. The penlight on her key ring didn't give off much light but at least she wouldn't be bumping into things.

"Ready?" She switched on the light. Jake moved in front and pressed his body against her legs.

"Okay," she said. "You go first."

Jake, with Stella close behind, skirted the tables and headed for the far side of the barn. When he reached the row of shops, he moved in close to the wall and stopped.

Stella spotted a glimmer of light showing around the entrance to one of the shops and aimed her penlight directly at the floor. She waited for Jake to move on.

Slowly, padding on silent paws, Jake approached the light. Stella crept forward, following. She placed one foot in front of the other slowly, making no sound on the concrete floor.

Jake stopped at the entrance and Stella moved up beside him. She reached out and parted the curtain, pulling it back far enough that she could peek into the shop. Krystal stood in the middle of the room, her back to the curtain and a pistol in her hand.

"I'm sorry, Kelly. I liked you. Really I did but this is something I had to do for my father. You can see that, can't you?" Jake took a flying leap into the shop and fastened his teeth onto her wrist. She squealed with pain and the gun clattered to the floor. Jake's weight hanging onto her arm brought her to her knees.

Stella ran across the room and grabbed the gun.

"Keep her covered!" Kelly shouted.

Jake stood, teeth bared in front of Krystal. He growled as he backed toward Kelly.

Stella stepped in front of Krystal, still holding the gun. "What were you doing? Were you going to kill all these people? It wasn't enough to kill your mother and your uncle?"

"Dear Stella!" Krystal spat the words. "As if you cared about them. The only thing that matters to you is money. Go ahead! Shoot me. Once I'm dead, you'll have it all."

Stella lowered the gun and backed away.

Krystal threw back her head and laughed. "I always knew you were a coward!" She whirled around and raced out of the shop.

"There's a knife on the counter." Kelly's voice brought Stella out of her shock.

"Oh, my God!" She ran to the counter and grabbed the knife, racing back to the rocking chair.

"Be careful," Kelly said. "The rope's wrapped around Penny's neck. You'll have to keep that section slack while you cut me loose."

Stella nodded and grasped the rope next to Kelly's hands. With a sawing motion, working slowly and using one hand to keep the rope that led to Penny slack, she worked through the strands until Kelly's hands were free.

"I'll see to Bubba." Kelly pulled the rope off his chest and got to his feet. "You get Penny loose."

"What about Krystal?"

"We haven't got time to worry about her. We've got to get these two out of here and get the paramedics."

"Is there a phone in here? Do you want me to call them?"

"No! Krystal planned on setting fire to this place and she might have another gas can. We need to get out of here. Now. We can call from the cabin. Do you think you can carry Penny?"

"Of course. She's only a little bit of a thing."

"Okay. Let's go then. Jake, you lead the way. I doubt if she'll try anything else." Kelly lifted Bubba to his shoulder and turned to Stella. "Be prepared, though, just in case. If Jake starts growling, lay Penny on the ground and get down yourself."

Stella nodded. She placed one arm under Penny's knees and the other around her back, lifting the sleeping girl into her arms. "I'm ready," she said.

Kelly switched on his flashlight and led the way out of the barn.

Outside, the clouds had cleared and the moon lit the path to the cabin. They made their way up the hill, slowly, with Jake in the lead. There was no sign of Krystal. Once inside the cabin, Kelly sent Stella to the bedroom with Penny while he stretched Bubba out on the couch and called 9-1-1.

"I don't like his color," he said when Stella came back into the room. "You just hang in there, little buddy." He covered Bubba with a blanket Stella brought from the bedroom. "Did you get hold of Gus?"

Stella shook her head. "His wife said she'd get him."

"That'd be Betty. She'll track him down. Do you want some coffee?"

Stella shook her head. "I couldn't swallow," she said in a choked voice.

Wordlessly, the two of them sat at the kitchen table until finally, the sound of approaching sirens reached their ears.

"Here they come." Kelly headed out to the porch.

Pandemonium broke loose within minutes. An emergency unit and two fire trucks screamed into the yard. Kelly'd just finished assisting them with the stretchers when Gus' official car, followed by two patrol cars, screeched into the yard. Kelly met him at his car.

"What's going on?"

"Krystal had Bubba and Penny trapped inside Anna's stall. They're both alive but Bubba's in pretty bad shape. I think she's still down there," Kelly said. "If you'll wait until they get Bubba and Penny transported, I'll show you."

"No." Gus shook his head. "We'll take it from here. You go along with the medics."

"Okay." Kelly accepted Gus' decision without comment. Given his previous relationship with Krystal, he shouldn't be involved in her apprehension.

"I'll see you at the hospital when it's over," Gus called after him.

Kelly nodded his head and walked over to join Stella. "We'll take the car and follow them in." Stella wordlessly handed over the keys.

Chapter Twenty-Three

Finally, after a couple of tense hours, Kelly was allowed to visit Bubba in his hospital room. The doctors had already assured him both Bubba and Penny would be fine given a couple of days to rest from their ordeal. When Kelly returned to the lobby he found Gus waiting with Stella.

"Did you find her?" Kelly asked and sank wearily into one of the chairs.

Gus nodded. "She's dead," he said.

Kelly's head jerked up in surprise. "How come?"

Gus shook his head. "We found her hanging from one of the beams. Looks like she went back into the stall after you'd left, took the rope she'd tied you and Penny with, wrapped it around her neck and tied it to the beam. Then she climbed up on the counter and jumped off."

"What a damn shame nobody figured out how twisted she was before it ever came to something like this."

"I know," Gus said. "I've just been telling Stella, there's nothing either one of you could've done to change the outcome. She got lost a long time ago and by the time anybody realized how bad she was, it was already way too late."

There wasn't much to say after that. Stella drove Kelly out to Indian Creek and when he offered a bed for the night, she thanked him for his offer but said she needed to get back home. There were still things that had to be dealt with concerning both Krystal and Andrew and she wouldn't be able to sleep in any event.

Kelly gave her a hug and promised to visit in the future. After she pulled out of the yard, he went into the cabin and fell onto his bed. He didn't bother to undress.

* * *

Two days later, after a long, dark session of soul-searching, Kelly was back at the Hideaway, ready to tie up the last loose end surrounding the death of his old friend, Anna.

"You okay?" Cam called across the room.

Kelly'd been staring blankly at the ceiling and shifted his attention to Cam. "Yeah, fine. How about giving Bubba a call and asking him to come over here and join us?"

"Sure thing!" Cam reached for the phone. He turned back to Kelly after he hung up. "He'll be right over."

"Good!" Kelly nodded and turned his attention to Cam.

The barman was antsy as a cricket on a hot griddle and Kelly figured it was time to put him out of his misery. "Why don't you grab a couple longnecks out of the cooler and come take a load off. I want to talk to both you and Bubba and I reckon you'd appreciate an update on your own situation."

"Coming right up." Cam practically danced over to the cooler.

Kelly leaned back in the booth and flexed his shoulder blades. He hoped he was doing the right thing about Frank. He had an idea how to handle the situation but he'd have to see what Bubba thought.

Cam slid into the booth and pushed a bottle across the table. "So what's up?" He fixed his anxious brown eyes on Kelly's face.

"Gus has talked to the DA," Kelly's face relaxed into a weary smile. "They've decided not to press the burglary charge."

Cam dropped his arms on the table. "You don't know what a load that takes off me," he said. "I've been heaving my guts out every time I thought about those charges."

"I know. It's been a rotten time for all of us but now that it's over maybe we can get back to some semblance of normalcy."

Cam nodded and heaved a sigh. "So where does that leaves things with Frank?"

"I take it he talked."

"Oh, yeah. The little weasel took the money all right."

"How'd you manage to sweat it out of him?"

Cam's grin was almost back to normal. "I invited him over to the house and fed him a couple dozen beers, then I laid it on thick about how he'd set himself up for a murder charge. Before I finished, I had him bawling like a baby."

"Was I right about his inheritance?"

"Yep. It was just like you figured. Frank was livid when he found out he wasn't even mentioned in his sister's will. He'd been expecting at least twenty grand. I think he'd already ordered the boat on his expectations. So when he overheard Anna telling me she'd put the fish camp money in her stash, it must've seemed made to order. He already knew her hiding place, so all he had to do was wait 'til she started in on the whiskey, then go help himself."

"How'd he know about her hiding place?"

Cam shrugged. "Snooping as usual. I guess he heard her mention it to Bubba one night and first chance he got, he snuck into her cabin and checked it out."

"Did he tell you when he took the money?"

"Yeah, it was while I was up on the bridge with Anna. He already had the box open when he heard our voices up on the bridge. He figured we were on our way over to the cabin, so he dropped everything and high-tailed it over to his boat."

"Little bastard," Kelly said.

"I know. I've already told him how much I appreciate his telling the cops about my fight with Anna. The son of a bitch was hoping they'd hang the robbery on me along with the murder."

"Hi, guys." Bubba strode in the door and called out a greeting. "What's up?" he asked, after he'd shuffled over to their table."

"You feeling okay?" Kelly slid into the booth to make room.

"Aw, sure!" Bubba reached up and touched the bandage covering the spot on his head where Krystal had whacked him with the board. "It's lucky she hit me on the head though. Otherwise, she might've done some serious damage."

Kelly grinned and clapped the little guy on the back. "We were just having a talk about Frank," he said, once Bubba had settled into the booth. "Cam says he's already told you about Frank taking Anna's money."

"Yeah! I'm not sure what we ought to do, though. It goes against my grain to turn anybody over to the cops. Even a snake like Frank."

"I figured as much," Kelly said. "That's what gave me this idea I've been mulling around."

"What idea is that?"

Kelly turned his head to include Cam in the conversation.

Then, with both their attention fixed, he turned back to Bubba.

"Now that Krystal's dead, you'll inherit under the terms of Anna's will, so the bulk of her estate, after a few bequests are paid off, belongs to you."

"So does that mean I can let Frank keep his stupid boat if I want to?" Bubba asked.

"Technically, yes." Kelly said. "He's guilty of theft and we ought to turn him in but I've got an idea that might appeal to you."

"I'm all ears." Bubba grinned and grabbed his ear.

"Seems to me it isn't right for Frank to get away with ripping off Anna's money but I agree with you, jail's not the answer," Kelly said. "So what I've been thinking is how about if you tell Frank you'll let him slide on the theft provided he donates both the boat and his services to the Indian Creek Boy Scouts."

Cam's black eyes popped. Unable to contain himself, he threw back his head and laughed.

"Hot damn!" Bubba yelped. "Frank'll be so busy with them kids, he won't have no time left to poke his nose into other folks' business."

Kelly grinned. "I kinda figured you'd cotton to that one."

"This calls for a beer," Cam stood up. "You ready for another one, Bubba?"

"You're damn right I am. I just wish Anna was here. She'd laugh her ass off at this plan of yours."

"Hey!" Kelly said. "Who's to say she's not looking down on us right now."

Bubba's eyes misted with tears. "I sure do miss the old gal."

"Let's have a toast." Cam set a tray of longnecks on the table and picked one up. The others did the same and all three bottles clinked mid-air.

"To Anna!"

The End

About the Author

Jude Pittman and her husband John live in Airdrie, Alberta. Retired after several decades of working in law firms, Jude now devotes her time to her love of Books.

Jude is one of the shareholder/owners of Books We Love Ltd. As an author she has published the romantic suspense novels Kelly McWinter PI *Deadly Secrets, Deadly Betrayal and Deadly Consequences*. In addition, Jude has published the novella *Healing Spirits, Bad Medicine* and co-written with author Gail Roughton, *Sisters of Prophecy: Ursula*, the first book in a paranormal, time travel, mystery series featuring Jude's ancestor, Mother Shipton a prophetess from 15th Century England.

Jude is currently at work on the 4th Kelly McWinter mystery, Deadly Lights. And Jude and Gail are working on Sisters of Prophecy: Irene

http://bookswelove.net/authors/pittman-jude/